SISTERS
of
ISIS

3

Enchantress

LYNNE EWING

HYPERION/NEW YORK

Published by Hyperion Books for Children, an imprint of
Disney Book Group. No part of this book may be reproduced
or transmitted in any form or by any means, electronic or
mechanical, including photocopying, recording, or by any
information or storage retrieval system, without written
permission from the publisher. For information, please address
Hyperion Books for Children, 114 Fifth Avenue, New York,
New York 10011-5690.

Printed in the United States of America
First Edition
1 3 5 7 9 10 8 6 4 2
This book is set in 12-point Griffo Classico.
Reinforced binding
Library of Congress Cataloging-in-Publication Data on file
ISBN-13: 978-1-4231-0684-5
ISBN-10: 1-4231-0684-9

www.hyperionteens.com

For Lyandra Géralmie Dervaux-Fitzgerald

Dalila feared she had made a terrible mistake. The worry kept nagging at her until she couldn't concentrate on anything her tutor, Mrs. Lavendish, was saying about the National Gallery of Art's exhibit on Netherlandish diptychs.

"Are you feeling ill, Dalila?" Mrs. Lavendish placed her hand on Dalila's forehead. When she lifted her arm, her blazer opened, exposing the gun in the holster cradled under her shoulder.

Dalila had recently learned that all her tutors

had actually been bodyguards, ex-FBI types hired by her uncle to protect her from the people who wanted to kill her.

Mrs. Lavendish frowned. "You're trembling."

"I forgot to eat breakfast," Dalila lied, suddenly seeing her chance to escape. The plan was risky, but she had to find out if she had done something unforgivable.

"We'll get a snack in the café," Mrs. Lavendish said in her most soothing voice.

Dalila hated to lie again, but she did. "Let me use the restroom first. I'll be right back."

"Alone?" Mrs. Lavendish looked puzzled. Dalila had never tried to go off by herself before. Someone always waited by the door for her.

"You stay and look at the . . ." Dalila had already forgotten what the tiny paintings were called.

Mrs. Lavendish adjusted her blazer. "I'll go with you."

"I won't be gone but a minute," Dalila answered peevishly. She couldn't tell Mrs. Lavendish the real reason she needed to be alone. But her abrupt tone stunned her tutor enough to gave Dalila the seconds she needed. She walked quickly away, though hopefully not so fast that Mrs. Lavendish would become alarmed and follow her.

When Dalila reached the rotunda, she darted into the checkroom. The attendant glanced at Dalila's number, then handed her a long rod inlaid with blue and green stones that mimicked the pattern on snakes' skin.

"I'm glad you came and got that thing." The attendant dropped it on the counter with a loud clank. "I swear I heard it hissing. What is it, anyway?"

"It's my magic wand," Dalila answered. Sometimes it was easier to tell the truth, especially when no one would believe you. She picked up the rod and nervously rubbed her fingers over the Egyptian hieroglyphs etched into the metal.

She left the museum and bounded down the front steps, then ducked and hid in the throng of tourists moving slowly toward the National Museum of Natural History. She had seldom been allowed out by herself and never in such a crowded public place. But since she had learned the truth about the meaning of her birthmark, she had become determined not to live such a sheltered life. After all, if she had to fight demons, then she should at least be allowed to go to parties and date.

A group of students in school uniforms crowded in front of her. They yelled and teased one another. Their play reminded Dalila of how much she had missed. She had been homeschooled, and her only companions had been adults. She had never had a friend her own age until recently.

She followed the young students across the Mall to the carousel, then leaned against the fence, listening to the mechanical bells and the jarring melody. Mothers and fathers held their small children on the circling horses. Their smiles and laughter opened a deep sadness inside Dalila. Her own parents had been killed in a cave-in while excavating a tomb in the Valley of the Kings when she was seven years old. Since that time she had lived with her uncle, the famous Egyptologist Anwar Serenptah. She loved him, but she needed her mother, especially now that she had so many questions about boys. Well, not "boys," exactly, just one, named Carter. Was it normal to feel so breathless when he put his arm around her? She thought of Carter, imagining the softness of his white-blond hair brushing across her face when he leaned down to kiss her.

A breeze caressed her. It was no more than a whisper of air, but it pulled her away from her thoughts, giving her the growing sense that someone was watching her. She stepped cautiously back onto the pebble-covered path. Yellow leaves fell from the branches overhead and fluttered to the ground. She glanced around, wondering if Mrs. Lavendish had followed her after all, but she didn't see her or anyone who could have explained the tingling in her back.

People passed, staring at her wand. Perhaps their curious glances had caused the uncomfortable feeling. Mrs. Lavendish had said that the wand looked like the ornamental scepter carried by rulers as a symbol of their sovereignty. That was close to the truth. The wand was supposed to be a symbol of her power as a magician, although she had no idea how to use it yet. For some reason, her mentor Abdel had been holding back, not telling her everything she needed to know. Most of what she knew about magic had come from her uncle, who had taught her the old ways. Maybe Abdel didn't think she was smart enough to learn the sacred knowledge. She hadn't really mastered the one power he had given her: the ability to transform.

Dalila shuddered just thinking about it. She detested snakes. She had always been afraid of them, and now she had the power to become one: a fire-breathing cobra.

She sighed, straightened her back, and began hiking toward the Washington Monument. She had always thought that she was living a sheltered life because she was being groomed to marry a Middle Eastern prince. From a young age she'd been told that her family was descended from the Egyptian pharaohs, but recently Abdel had told her the true meaning of her birthmark: she was a Descendant, destined to stand against evil and defend the world. She still couldn't believe that her uncle hadn't told her the truth.

She increased her pace, walking faster and holding her wand like a shepherd's staff, tapping it hard on the ground. She repeated the words that Abdel had spoken over her to awaken the soul of Egypt lying dormant within her: "Sublime of magic, your heart is pure. To you I send the power of the ages. Divine one, come into being."

Just saying the words made her nerves thrum the way they had that first night. Abdel had told her that, back in ancient times, the goddess Isis had given the Hour priests the Book of Thoth and instructed them to watch the night skies. When the stars warned of danger, the priests were supposed to give the book to the pharaoh, so he could use its magic to protect the world.

Nowadays, the Hour priests met as a secret society. When they learned that the Cult of Anubis had moved to Washington, D.C., they sent Abdel to find the Descendants born with the sacred birthmark. Only the divine heirs had the power to use the magic in the Book of Thoth. Dalila hoped that was true, because so far, she and the two girls Sudi and Meri, who had been summoned with her, hadn't done a very good job.

Their task was made more difficult because residents in the District thought the cult was a new age group from California. Authorities would never believe the truth: the cult leaders worshipped the evil god Seth and used Anubis and the Book of

Gates in unholy ways, to call forth demons and resurrect the dead. More than likely, if Dalila did go to the police, she'd end up with a court-ordered visit to a psychiatrist.

She crossed Fourteenth Street, her nervousness growing, as she followed the trail between the tall pine trees. Soon she was passing the Bureau of Engraving and Printing. To her right, the Tidal Basin glimmered in the late afternoon sun. She had a sudden vision of a hellish monster rising from the water and pulling her back under with it.

Some weeks before, she had tossed a papyrus containing a powerful spell into the water. The hieroglyphs had dissolved, but had the magic? Ancient Egyptians had viewed magic, *heka*, as the energy of creation, a power unto itself, and that had begun her worries. If she had freed something evil, then she had to find a way to capture it before the cult found out what she had done.

She dreaded telling Abdel. She knew she should have been more cautious, but at the time she had wanted only to destroy the incantation. Her motives were right, but unfortunately the outcome might prove disastrous. She took a deep breath, fighting her uneasiness, and headed down to the Tidal Basin.

When she was certain no one was watching her, she leaned over the railing and stirred the water with the tip of her wand. Ripples spread over the surface in lazy waves, but nothing more happened. The tension that had been building in her muscles gave way, and she began to relax. She had expected the hieroglyphs on the wand to move, but they lay still beneath her fingers. Maybe her worries had been for nothing after all.

An unexpected gust of wind startled her. She cried out and almost dropped her wand. She caught it, fumbled with it, and tried to hold on. The wand clanked noisily against the railing as she pulled it back toward her.

Finally she held it firmly in her hands, but she didn't understand why the blast of wind had frightened her so. Her heart was still hammering, and she had an odd sense of foreboding that made her uneasy. She winced just imagining what would have happened if she had dropped the wand in the water. How could she ever have explained that to Abdel?

When she looked up again, an ugly, stout man stood near her. A scraggly tuft of hair grew from his chin, although the rest of his face was clean-shaven. His eyebrows met at the bridge of his nose, and in the slanted light his eyes looked curiously orange, the black pupils rectangular instead of round. He blinked, and she realized it must have been the reflection of morning sunlight that had caused the illusion: his eyes were deep green.

Still, his abrupt appearance confused her. Surely she would have noticed him joining her, or heard him scuffling through the dead leaves that covered the walkway. She gave him a tentative smile.

The man glared in response.

She turned away, self-conscious, and plucked at her hair. Maybe he was staring at the birthmark near her temple. The sacred eye of Horus identified her as a Descendant but also marked her for death. Since she had learned the truth, she had tried to keep it hidden, but the wind might have blown back her hair and uncovered it.

"I know who you are already." The man's words tore through her.

When she glanced back at him, she saw no friendliness in his fixed stare.

"Come with me, Dalila." He held out his thick callused hand.

"Who are you?" She hesitated, not sure how he knew her name. Maybe he was yet another bodyguard hired by her uncle to make sure she didn't do anything foolish. It wouldn't be the first time a new chaperone had suddenly appeared to watch over her. She supposed he could have followed her out of the museum, especially if her uncle had hired an additional guard to make sure she didn't do something exactly like this.

But when she held the man's gaze, fear and repulsion made her step back.

"Dalila," he said sternly. "Don't make me come after you."

"Did my uncle send you to find me?" she asked.

"Of course," he answered. "How else would I know your name?"

She had been trained to accommodate tutors, chaperones and bodyguards. She overrode her feeling of loathing for the man—besides it wasn't right to judge people by their appearance alone—and started toward him.

But with her first step, her wand throbbed against her palm. The hieroglyphs came alive, gibbering anxiously and re-forming, moving in a stream too fast for her to read.

She stopped.

In the same moment, the man lifted his hand. When he brought it down, a flock of black birds was startled into flight. Glossy wings flapped over Dalila's face. She dropped the wand and covered her eyes, shrieking.

When quiet returned, she peeked out through her fingers. Feathers were fluttering around her, and the wand lay at her feet, the hieroglyphs no longer moving.

"You're to come with me." The man caught a feather and with a flourish waved it back and forth. A tremulous light grew between the lines where the feather had marked the air and then settled over her. She grimaced. The unnatural heaviness forced her down on the ground next to her wand. She gasped, unable to breathe, the pain in her back excruciating as she fought the force. She managed to clutch her wand and hold on to it with both hands. It was her only hope.

The man chuffed with satisfaction and stepped toward her through the leaves piled along the sidewalk.

As the pressure surrounding her eased, she tensed her body, getting ready. Even though Abdel hadn't shown her how to use the wand's magic, the rod itself had the lethal weight of a weapon.

When the man was close enough, she jumped up and swung.

He ducked, then stumbled back, losing his balance. He flung his arms out and hit the ground with a loud grunt.

Dalila bolted and ran up the path that led to the street. She didn't know who the man was, but he hadn't been sent by her uncle. More likely he belonged to the cult.

The hollow clopping of a horse's hooves made her glance back. She didn't understand what had made the sound, but she couldn't stop and investigate, because the man had recovered and was chasing her. He huffed and snorted noisily.

She darted into the oncoming traffic. Tires squealed. Horns blared. Cars swerved and whooshed around her, leaving dirty air and fumes in their wake. She held her hand over her nose and stood on the narrow concrete divide in the middle of the road, not sure what to do.

The man was not relenting, and she had thought he would once she scrambled onto the road where there would be witnesses to his pursuit. She looked frantically around for a way to escape. She could never make it back to the art gallery and find Mrs. Lavendish before the man caught her. Mrs. Lavendish would be looking for her, but what hope did she have that her tutor would locate her here before the man seized her? She had to rely on her own cunning. She needed to hide.

She dashed back across the street, recklessly dodging two speeding cars, and sprinted across the bridge and down the curving path toward the Jefferson Memorial.

As soon as the traffic sounds were behind her, Dalila realized her mistake. The area was too deserted. She stepped under the twiggy, low-hanging branches on the cherry trees. Her shoes incantation that Abdel had given her. "Make a path for me to change my earthly *khat* into that of your divine Wadjet."

Energy quivered through her. She couldn't stop now. The metamorphosis had begun.

She completed the spell. "*Xu kua.* I am glorious. *User Kua.* I am mighty. *Neteri kua.* I am strong."

Her muscles cramped. Dull pain throbbed through her bones. Then, greenish black scales raced over her skin with an odd tickle, one overlapping the next. Her body twisted out of its normal shape, winding and coiling until she fell to the ground, a sleek cobra.

Her tongue flicked out, and, as a snake, she tasted the air. The man's scent terrified her. Instinctively, she reared up, spreading the skin of her neck into a hood. Why did the man make her feel so afraid?

She swayed, ready to strike, then caught herself and let her head fall back onto the damp soil.

The vibrations from the man's footsteps pounded through her.

As she watched him, a new worry took hold. Even though she could see him with her eyes, she squished in the mud, leaving a trail. She quickly jumped onto some dried grass and leaves.

The constant shift between shadow and dazzling sunlight blinded her. She blinked, trying to see. At last, she slipped behind a thick tree trunk and listened.

Silence followed.

Maybe she had lost the man after all. She pressed her cheek against the rough bark and peeked out.

He stood near the water, hands on his hips, peering into the dark beneath the gnarled trees.

She jerked her head back and hoped he hadn't seen her. Her body trembled with uncontrollable fear as her mind raced, trying to come up with a plan. She had only one way to escape. Cautiously, she crept across the grass and ducked beneath a holly tree. The thorny leaves scratched her face and hands, but the branches met the ground and concealed her well enough for the moment. She clutched the wand close to her body, hoping it would disappear with her.

"Amun-Re, eldest of the gods in the east sky, mysterious power of wind." She whispere was unable to perceive him using the sensors in the small pits on either side of her head that normally created images from the heat emitted by the objects surrounding her. She switched back and forth between her two systems, astonished. The man gave off no warmth. Maybe he was an apparition, or worse, one of the walking dead sent by the Cult of Anubis. But why did he want her to go with him when it would have been so much easier just to destroy her?

"Dalila?" He paused near the holly tree. The branches began to shudder, and the red berries trembled. He was making the air pulse oddly.

She slithered under decayed leaves into sloshing mud, certain the man was using some kind of supernatural radar to find her. She lay motionless, taking in the cold of the ground.

Finally, the man edged back toward the water. He paused twice to study the shadows, and then he was gone.

His heavy steps no longer vibrated through her. The only quiver in the earth came from the traffic speeding over the bridge. Still, she remained hiding, in case the man was trying to trick her.

At last, she slid out of the mud and straightened until she stood upright on the tip of her tail. Then she began spinning and continued to twirl until her arms, legs, and head re-formed. When she stopped, she was a girl again. The world tilted and spun.

It always took a few seconds for her to feel normal after her transformation back, but this time something was wrong. Her vision was muzzy, her thoughts disoriented, but most of all, she felt incredibly dizzy and cold. Her hand clasped the wand, and, using it like a walking stick, she took one clumsy step forward and swayed. She stumbled out into bright morning sunlight as another wave of vertigo washed over her.

When she tripped and started to fall, strong hands caught her waist before she hit the ground. She hadn't escaped the man after all.

CHAPTER 2

Dalila tried to run, but her legs were too numb, her strength gone. She still held the wand, and she swung it now, but it only wobbled in her frozen hands. She surrendered and began shivering violently.

"Dalila." A familiar voice called her name. Carter held her. "What's wrong?" She relaxed against him, but her teeth chattered, and she couldn't move her lips to answer his question. Even if she had been able to speak, she couldn't have told him the truth. And would he have believed her if she confessed that just minutes before, she had been a snake, a cold-blooded creature that relied on an outside source for warmth? She was lucky she wasn't in a complete stupor.

"What happened?" Carter brushed his hand over her hair. Leaves and dirt fell to her shoulders and onto the ground.

She glanced down. Her sweater was covered with mud. Abdel had to teach her how to transform correctly before something tragic happened. This time she had come back covered with mud, but what if she had returned with scales instead of skin? She could end up a freak in a sideshow.

Carter took off his bulky gray jacket and placed it over her shoulders. She nestled herself inside the warm lining, and her muscles began to relax. The shivering stopped, and her vision returned, but then she became aware of the residue of the man's smell, lingering as a sickening taste in her mouth. She needed to spit.

"Are you going to be sick?" Carter asked with concern.

She shook her head no. Then she bent over and retched.

When she was finished, Carter held her in his arms and scanned the shadows beneath the trees. "You need to tell me what happened."

She stared at him, wondering why he looked so terrified. She could feel the tension in his body. Maybe he sensed something odd that made him wary. Or perhaps he had just watched too much nightly news and feared something horrible had happened to her.

"I'd better take you home." Without waiting for her permission, he lifted her up into his arms and walked toward the Jefferson Memorial. Leaves crackled beneath his feet.

She rested her head against his shoulder, enjoying the smell of his cologne, and gripped her wand tightly. "How did you find me?"

"Love," he teased, kissing the tip of her nose. When he pulled back, dirt was smeared across his lips and chin.

"Seriously, why were you here?" She tried to wipe the dirt off his face but only succeeded in making it worse.

"I told you," he said playfully. "Don't you believe in the power of my love?"

She knew he was attempting to make her laugh, but terror wasn't a state of mind so easily shaken. She tried to concentrate on Carter, his amazing good looks, his easy smile, but her thoughts kept jumping back to the man who had made her feel so afraid.

By the time Carter had circled the memorial, warmth had returned to her body. Even so, he carried her the remaining distance up to the street. His silver BMW was parked near a refreshment kiosk.

Carter set her down. "Now, tell me what you were doing," he said as he unlocked the car door.

"I ran away from my chaperone. It was such a beautiful morning." She couldn't continue the lie, but she couldn't tell him the truth, either. She looked away and stared at the planes taking off from Reagan Airport.

"Promise me you'll never do something so risky again," he said. "You're not used to being out on your own, and I bet you don't even have any money on you."

She realized how foolish she had been. How had she planned to get home?

He opened the car door and took her wand from her. When he touched it, the hieroglyphs became agitated and jumped. Dalila tried to read their message, but Carter tossed the wand into the back. It hit the seat with a soft thump.

She started to get into the car, but paused. A small, narrow box wrapped in silver paper and tied with a red bow sat on the passenger seat.

"It's for you," Carter whispered.

"Me?" She picked it up, surprised, and fell back against his chest. But when she pulled at the ribbon, a thought came to her. "How did you know you'd find me here?"

"I didn't." His hands reached impatiently around her. He took the present from her, tore off the paper, and opened the lid.

"Ooh," she breathed with delight. A bracelet lay inside: a single gold heart on a chain.

He took it out, letting the box fall to the ground, then fastened the chain around her wrist. When he was finished, he lifted the charm with the tip of his finger and held it up for her to read. The words *I love you* were engraved on the heart.

He nuzzled her ear, not caring about the dirt

clinging to her. "You know it's true," he whispered, his breath tickling her face. "But you don't have to tell me yet. Only when you're sure you feel the same way about me."

She wanted to tell him, but she was afraid. Sudi had told her that Carter had a reputation at Lincoln High for being a heartbreaker. Girls warned each other not to get involved, even though most of them were crushing on him themselves.

Dalila studied the charm and wondered how many other girls had received similar gifts from him.

"I never led anyone on," Carter said, seeming to sense her thoughts.

Her head whipped around. "How did you know—?"

"What you were thinking?" he finished for her. "You're frowning when you should be smiling at your new bracelet."

She tried to smile, but her lips stretched in a poor imitation of happiness.

"I was always honest with them," he went on, wiping the dirt from his face with the sleeve of his sweater. "The other girls knew I didn't love them.

Maybe they thought they could make me love them, but sex isn't love, Dalila."

"A person who wanted to deceive me would speak the same words." She immediately wished she had kept her doubts to herself. She could tell from his look that she had hurt him. "I'm sorry," she whispered, but it was too late: she had already spoiled the moment.

"Maybe someday you'll trust me." He shrugged and helped her into the car.

She watched him walk around to the driver's side. Something felt wrong. She didn't understand how he could be so unfazed—he had discovered her mud-covered, shivering, and unable to talk. She felt certain that if *she* had found *him* disoriented and filthy, she would have barraged him with a thousand questions until she knew exactly what had happened.

He slid behind the steering wheel, then caught her gaze. "What now?" he asked and smiled.

"Why were you at the Tidal Basin?" she asked.

The smile fell from his face, and he turned the key in the ignition. "You know I go jogging there," he replied.

The engine rumbled nicely, and heat blasted from the vents.

"But you should have been in school," she said. "It's still early."

She glanced down at his shoes and knew he was lying. He didn't wear leather loafers to run. He shifted in his seat, then turned up the music so she couldn't ask him more questions. The bass thumped through her, and the car zipped away.

By the time they pulled into the circular drive in front of her home in Chevy Chase, she had decided that Carter had probably gone down to the Tidal Basin to jog, but hadn't had a chance to change into his running shoes because he had seen her stagger out from her hiding place beneath the holly tree. And maybe the package containing the bracelet had been sitting on the passenger's seat for days, just waiting until he could surprise her. That was what she told herself, anyway. That was what she wanted to believe. She ignored the fact that he should have been in school.

At the front door, she turned to face him. "I'm going to be in trouble for running away from Mrs. Lavendish, so maybe it's better if you don't come in."

He nodded. "I'll call you this afternoon."

But she didn't really want him to go. She clasped his wrist and playfully pulled him back to her. She leaned her wand against the door frame, so that both her hands were free.

"Thank you for the bracelet." Without thinking, she slipped her arms around his waist. She had been so eager for his embrace, and now she felt suddenly shy. She looked down, embarrassed by her boldness, and wondered if he knew how strongly she felt about him. Her body tingled with pleasant sensations when she thought about kissing him, but at the moment it was betraying her with a blush.

He lifted her chin to make sure she was looking at him. "I love you, Dalila, and I've never said those words to another girl."

Then he kissed her. She let her hands slide up his back, delighting in the warm feel of his body. She didn't pull away, even when she heard the front door opening behind her. Her wand fell and rattled against the bricks.

"Dalila!" her uncle shouted angrily.

She spun around and wiped her lips, trying to

erase what she had just done. She had expected Mrs. Lavendish to be behind the door, not her uncle. It was too early for him to be home.

"So this is why you snuck away from Mrs. Lavendish," her uncle fumed.

"Carter found me." She fumbled with her words, trying to find the right ones to defuse her uncle's anger. "He helped me."

"Inside, now!" her uncle said sternly. He gently pushed her into the house, then turned to face Carter. "I told you to stay away from her."

Dalila glanced at her uncle, surprised. She didn't know he had spoken to Carter before—and at the same time she couldn't believe that Carter hadn't told her about their conversation.

"I know who you are and what you do," her uncle went on. "And this time I'm warning you: Stay away from Dalila."

Dalila wondered how her uncle had learned about Carter's reputation, but then, if he had hired bodyguards to protect her, he had probably paid someone to investigate Carter. Still, that seemed extreme, even for someone as old-fashioned and conservative as her uncle.

Carter held her uncle's gaze. "I love her, sir. I'd never do anything to harm her. I swear."

"On what do you swear?" her uncle asked darkly.

The odd question seemed to defeat Carter. He turned and hurried back to his car.

"Don't go." Dalila started after him.

Her uncle caught her wrist. "Don't shame yourself."

The car drove out onto the street and sped away.

CHAPTER 3

Dalila wanted to scream and cry and storm about her bedroom. Instead, she peeled off her muddy clothes, left them in a pile near her canopied bed, and stomped into her bathroom. She stood under the shower spray, letting the hot water wash away her tears. When her chest and throat ached from sobbing, she lathered with soap, rinsed, then shut off the water and wrapped herself in a giant pink towel.

She dressed in a cashmere sweater and gray

wool slacks. But as she passed her dresser and caught a glimpse of herself in the mirror, a spirit of rebellion made her stop. She tore off her conservative clothes and pulled on tight-fitting, bronze-studded jeans, a T, and her beaded velour hoodie.

She glanced at her reflection again, and, this time satisfied, she headed downstairs to face her uncle.

He was waiting for her in the living room, sipping tea from a small crystal glass. She caught a whiff of mint and knew he was drinking *chai bil na'ana* to calm his stomach. Immediately she wished she had stayed in the old-fashioned clothes that he had picked out for her. She didn't mean to cause him stress; she just wanted to be herself—but she wasn't even sure she knew who that was anymore.

He set the glass aside and stood. "Come with me."

She dutifully followed him down the hallway. Portraits of relatives she had never met hung in gilded frames on the long stretch of wall.

Her uncle was Anwar Serenptah, a world-renowned Egyptologist. His documentaries had appeared on the Discovery Channel, and he had received awards for his many books. But he always reminded Dalila that his most important and cherished responsibility was that of caring for her. He had trained her to become the perfect heir.

Her uncle unlocked the door to his study and held it open.

She entered, feeling a mix of curiosity and dread. He rarely let her into the room. Perhaps he wanted to talk to her in private, which meant he was far angrier than she had realized. The aroma of his pipe tobacco lingered in the air. Dust covered his desk and bookshelves and formed little balls at the carpet's edge. He didn't allow the housekeeper into the room to clean. Even so, his telescopes, one in each of the three floor-to-ceiling windows, gleamed in the late-morning sun, their lenses carefully covered.

Dalila pushed aside a stack of papers, then sat down on the worn plaid couch and waited for his lecture.

Her uncle fell into his leather chair and let out a tired sigh. He'd had a heart attack three years ago and his health had been fragile ever since. He looked older than his fifty years; he had never married, and she wondered if he had regrets that he hadn't had a family of his own, especially now that she was being so difficult.

He picked up his pipe, stuck it between his lips, and took a few puffs on the unlit tobacco, savoring it. Then he struck a wooden kitchen match and passed the flame over the top of the bowl. Sweet-scented smoke rose and formed thin, drifting vapors over his head.

At last he looked at Dalila, and the disappointment on his face made her cringe.

"I'm sorry I ran away from Mrs. Lavendish," she said quietly, hoping to ease the tension between them. "But I didn't do it so I could meet Carter."

"Dalila, I have to leave for Egypt tonight," he said, ignoring her apology. "The archeologists have uncovered some astonishing artifacts. I'm sure it's someone's idea of a joke. Still, I must go. . . ." He stopped and stared at the bracelet.

"Carter gave it to me." She held her breath, expecting him to tell her to take it off.

His eyes returned to hers. "Wear it always, as a reminder not to do anything foolish."

She looked down, blushing with embarrassment and shame. Did her uncle know the things she imagined doing with Carter?

"I can't delay my departure for Egypt." He set his pipe in a tray with a soft tap, then braced his hands on the desk and raised himself up. He took three slow steps toward the window and dropped to his knees.

Panicked, Dalila ran to him. She kneeled beside him, her hand reaching for his wrist to measure his pulse.

He looked up, surprised, and then his expression softened. "I'm all right, Dalila. I'm not having another heart attack. I should have shown you this a long time ago." He pulled back the edge of the carpet and then removed three short floorboards. They clattered against one another as he tossed them aside.

A safe with a combination lock lay underneath the floor. The dial clicked as he turned it. He opened it and drew out a small golden box.

"*Hery Seshta*." Dalila read the hieroglyphs on the lid. "Did the box once belong to a master magician?"

"The box and what it contains have been in our family since ancient times," he answered.

She stared at him.

"We kept the old ways even when it became against the law." He used the arm of a nearby chair to pull himself up. Then he carried the box back to his desk and set it down.

Dalila got up and stood across from him, anxious to see what lay inside.

Carefully, her uncle removed the lid. Something old and unbidden rushed out from inside, stirring dust motes and causing the papers on the bookshelves to flutter. Dalila breathed in the stale, musty odor and felt the presence of powerful magic. She glanced at her uncle and became uneasy. He seemed frightened and uncertain, but when he caught her gaze, his expression changed to one of deep pity and sorrow. He had looked at her that way the day he told her about her parents' deaths.

Her heart began beating faster, and she knew she didn't want to hear what he was going to say next. She tried to swallow, but her throat was too dry.

"I can't delay my departure for Egypt," her

uncle said, "and I'm afraid to leave you alone without protection."

"You've left me before," she argued, her voice jagged with anxiety. "And Mrs. Lavendish—"

"Mrs. Lavendish doesn't understand the real threat," he interrupted and went on. "And, of course, I can't tell her." He pulled a small piece of papyrus from inside the box and handed it to Dalila.

The fibers felt brittle and dry against her fingers. She carefully unrolled the papyrus and studied the writing.

"Use the incantation only if you find yourself in terrible danger and need to escape," her uncle explained.

She held the papyrus reverently. Only a small percentage of ancient Egyptians had been fully literate, and written magic had been prized and sought after. Spells were treasured and handed down within families. She thought of the generations of magicians before her who had held this same incantation in their hands, and she wondered what their lives had been. Then another thought came to her. "Why are you giving this to me now?"

"I study the stars," he said. "We've discussed this already, many times."

But he had never told her what he saw when he gazed at the night sky.

"Astronomers see stars and planets, but what do you see?" she asked. "What does the night sky tell you?"

He shook his head. "Keep the spell with you always."

He sounded tired and old. Normally she would have had a million questions, but this time she was more concerned about his health. He didn't seem well enough to travel.

"Maybe you should wait a day. You look too tired to take the trip," she ventured. "Surely no discovery is worth risking your health."

"I would have left already if I could have found a better flight." He picked up his pipe. "This can't wait."

She looked down at the small papyrus and started to read the writing aloud. When she uttered the first word, her uncle dropped his pipe. Cinders and ash exploded into the air as he stumbled around the desk. He clamped his hand over her mouth.

"You must never say the words unless your life is at risk," he said. "Promise me."

She could feel the trembling in his fingers and see the fear in his unblinking gaze. She nodded and he dropped his hold.

"Why are you giving me this if you're afraid of the magic it contains?" she asked.

"Because the Cult of Anubis has grown stronger than I ever imagined possible," he whispered in a dry, frightened tone. "And now that you have been summoned, I can't protect you the way I once did. You must rely on sorcery."

Dalila looked down at the papyrus again, feeling lost.

CHAPTER 4

Back in her bedroom, Dalila snuggled under her silky comforter. She wanted to spend the rest of the day in bed feeling sorry for herself, but she resolutely pushed that idea away. Happiness was a choice—or, at least, that was what Mrs. Lavendish had taught her—and right now she knew one person who could make her smile. She found her phone and speed-dialed Carter.

His voice came on: "You know the routine." A beep followed.

"I was hoping I could speak to you," Dalila began, not sure what to say. "Please call me." She hung up, dissatisfied.

Doubt began niggling at the back of her mind. She didn't understand why Carter hadn't answered his phone . . . unless he had seen the caller ID and didn't want to speak to her. Maybe she had always been just another trophy, and after her uncle's outburst he had decided that she was no longer worth—

"Stop." She tried to gain control over her emotions. Then, with a flash of happiness, she thought of her new friends, Sudi and Meri, and realized she was no longer alone. She picked up the phone again and dialed Sudi's number.

"It's me," Dalila said. "Can you come over?"

In less than an hour, Sudi stood in front of Dalila's dresser, running a flat iron through her long blond hair. "What we really need is some chocolate," Sudi said. "A sugar high will always make you feel better. That's my number one breakup rule—and I should know, because I'm a total magnet for heartbreak."

"Please," Meri argued. "Guys line up just begging for a chance to date you."

"That doesn't mean the *right* one is asking," Sudi retorted.

Meri sat on her skateboard, rolling from side to side, wheels squeaking as she examined Dalila's muddy clothes. Meri's mother—a senator from California who planned to become the first woman president—had hired a stylist to make her daughter look more suitable. But Meri had kept her beach style: she wore leggings under the skirt of her private-school uniform, and Converse tennis shoes instead of the regulation oxfords.

Sudi went to public school at Lincoln High. She wore a slouchy pencil skirt with the last three buttons undone to show off her legs, and a skinny polo.

"Trust me." Sudi began applying liquid eyeliner to her lids. "I know about breaking up."

"Ewww!" Meri squealed and pointed to an earthworm crawling in the dirt that was caked on Dalila's wool sweater. "If Carter kissed you when you were looking like a swamp monster, then he must love you. What happened?"

"Carter and I didn't 'break up,' exactly," Dalila said.

Meri rolled closer. "Give us the details."

Sudi kicked off her ankle boots and crawled onto the bed next to Dalila.

"My uncle said I wasn't allowed to see him anymore," Dalila said.

"Why?" Meri asked.

"He thought I ran away from Mrs. Lavendish so I could meet Carter down at the Tidal Basin," Dalila explained.

"My mom said some of the walkways were flooded," Sudi said. "Is that how you got so muddy?"

"Not exactly." Dalila hesitated, wondering how much she should tell them.

"Are you going to keep seeing him?" Meri asked. "You are, aren't you? I can see it in your eyes. Dalila, you were such a goody-goody. I can't believe you're becoming one of the bad girls."

"What is this power that Carter has over girls?" Sudi asked.

"You're just immune to him because he's your friend," Meri said. "He's amazingly cute, and he has this curious way about him. . . . He just has this smoldering look that makes you want to kiss him. I mean, that makes Dalila want to kiss him."

Dalila laughed. She knew that Meri wasn't crushing on Carter—she was too busy being totally infatuated with Abdel, their mentor.

"So?" Sudi stood and picked up one of the perfumes on Dalila's dresser. She sprayed it in her hair. The scent of rose and musk filled the room. "What are you going to do?"

"I can't betray my uncle," Dalila said, although technically she already had when she had left the message for Carter. "What should I do?"

"I hated that Carter was with you," Sudi confessed. "I was worried that—"

"Nothing happened," Dalila said, then paused, becoming thoughtful. "No, that's not true."

Meri looked shocked. "You did something and you didn't tell us?"

"Not *that*," Dalila said. "I think I fell in love with him." Dalila blinked away her tears. "How can I ever forget him? I know I can't."

"Dalila, we ditched school and came over here to cheer you up," Sudi said. "And that's what we're going to do." She put a CD in the player and turned up the volume. The haunting, flutelike music of a Kawala played. The high-pitched notes were joined by the metal sound of cymbals on the mazhar.

"You love to play this music when you teach us how to belly dance," Sudi said. "Now, watch out." Sudi pulled up her shirt, exposing her flat stomach, and tried to do a belly roll, her ab muscles tightening and releasing in waves.

Her awkward motion made Dalila smile.

Meri jumped up and thrust her hips out the way Dalila had taught them.

When Dalila giggled, Sudi and Meri kept it up, purposely bumping into each other until Dalila was laughing so hard she clutched her pillow, out of breath.

Meri stopped abruptly and turned off the music.

"What's wrong?" Sudi asked. "I was just getting into it." She shimmied one last time.

Dalila sat up. "Why did you stop?"

Meri studied Dalila, a puzzled look on her face. "But, Dalila, if you didn't go down to the Tidal Basin to see Carter, then why did you run away from Mrs. Lavendish?"

Dalila looked from one friend to the other, then said, "I think I made a terrible mistake." She grew somber. "Remember the night we tried to summon Seth? I threw the papyrus with the incantation into the water."

"That was the right thing to do," Sudi said. "We didn't want the cult to use the magic and possibly destroy the world."

"Then I began thinking," Dalila said. "What if the magic didn't disappear with the hieroglyphs? What if I freed something dangerous?"

"You mean, like, something was imprisoned by the writing? Something capable of acting on its own?" Meri looked worried, and Dalila wondered if she had already had similar thoughts.

"It was just a spell that we recited," Sudi argued. "You're worrying about nothing."

"But what power do spoken words have?" Dalila asked. "There must be some form of energy behind the incantation that brings about the change."

"It's magic," Sudi answered with a shrug.

"Magic is a force," Meri said, seeming to agree with Dalila.

"And when we speak an incantation," Dalila continued, "maybe we're binding a force to do our bidding. Something changes when we cast a spell, and what brings about that change? Perhaps, thousands of years ago, an ancient entity was chained to the incantation on the papyrus—"

"You mean it was locked up inside the fibers?" Sudi looked doubtful.

"Not exactly, but close," Dalila said. "Meri told us that a black shadow was surrounding the two of us."

"I don't like where this is going," Sudi said dolefully. "I'm still not over our last adventure."

"What if the shadow was the force that was controlled by the spell, and when I threw the papyrus into the water—"

"—The hieroglyphs dissolved, and the energy was freed," Meri finished for her.

"Something powerful enough to summon the evil god Seth," Sudi whispered, looking nervous.

"So you went down to the Tidal Basin to find out," Meri concluded. "But did you see anything?"

Dalila looked down at her hands, wondering if she should tell them about the man who had chased her. In hindsight, she thought he had probably been no more than one of the many homeless people in D.C. After all, she had lived a lonely life, without friends her own age, and to compensate, she had developed a huge imagination to entertain herself. Perhaps the man had been more daydream than threat, his magic no more than a fusion of her hysteria and fear.

"Maybe we should visit Abdel," Dalila said at last.

When she glanced up, Sudi and Meri were already pulling on their coats.

CHAPTER 5

By the time the girls got off the bus in Georgetown, thin clouds had slipped over the sky, and a cold wind had come down from the northwest. They walked up the hill, red leaves skittering around them in the wood smoke–scented air.

"I hope he's home," Dalila said when they stopped in front of the yellow row house where Abdel lived.

Sudi shrugged. "Even if he is, it's not like he's going to tell us anything we need to know."

"Then why did we bother to come?" Meri whined, her breath a wisp of white vapor. "He's going to think I put you up to this because I wanted to see him."

"Don't you?" Sudi elbowed her playfully.

"Of course I do—except, at a party, not here." Meri tugged nervously at her gloves. "I really like him—but as a mentor, he's about as good as a math teacher who can't count."

"He belongs to the Hour priests," Dalila said, not sure why she was defending him. "So he must have done something important once to become a member."

"He warned us that he probably wasn't the best priest to advise us," Meri added. "I just wish he was a regular guy and someone else was our teacher."

"This time he has to help us." Sudi grinned slyly. "Because we won't leave until he does."

Dalila clasped the iron handrail and dashed up the steps. "Maybe he can at least tell us if I set the magic free."

Meri followed close behind her. "Don't blame

yourself. We all thought destroying the papyrus was the right thing to do."

"Did you ever wonder if maybe the reason he doesn't tell us anything is because he's testing us to see if we're worthy?" Dalila asked as she knocked on the door.

Meri took off her glove and held up her hand, flaunting her ring. The sacred eye of Horus was fashioned in the gold band with lapis lazuli and green faience. Each of the girls wore one. "If the goddess Isis thinks we're good enough and even gave us her rings, then I think we passed the test already."

"Then why aren't we good enough for Abdel?" Dalila asked anxiously.

Abdel opened the door. He didn't look surprised to see them, but he didn't invite them inside, either.

"We're . . . we're here. . . ." Dalila stammered, trying to explain why they needed to speak to him, but Sudi crowded in front of her.

"We're here," Sudi said. "Deal with it." She pushed past Abdel and flopped into one of the overstuffed armchairs in the living room.

Meri followed her. Dalila hurried inside to the hearth and stretched out her hands, trying to warm her numb fingers. The fire crackled, and embers shot into the air.

Abdel closed the door and joined them, his footsteps hollow on the floor. He sat down on a bench.

No one spoke until, finally, Abdel broke the silence. "I suppose there is something important that you need to tell me." His tone implied that he already knew about and disapproved of what they had done.

"I think I made a mistake," Dalila began. Her chin quivered, but not from the cold. How could Abdel make her so nervous? He was her age and had no authority over her. He was supposed to help her.

"It wasn't just Dalila." Meri came to her defense. "I told you that we were trying to call forth Seth so we could stop Apep."

Abdel nodded. "That was a foolish mistake."

"But Apep was killing tourists!" Sudi blurted. "And you weren't there to tell us what to do."

Dalila shot a warning glance at Sudi. They

couldn't risk arguing with Abdel and making him angry when they needed information from him.

"Fortunately, Meri stopped us in time," Dalila added, forcing a smile.

"The three of you had promised me that you wouldn't act on your own," Abdel reminded them angrily. "What you did was dangerous. Even the smallest ritual, when done without thought, can have unexpected complications." He paused and took several deep breaths. Then he continued, "You stopped reciting the spell before it was completed. And then you failed to speak another spell to deactivate the magic that you had started to open." He scowled and looked at each one of them before going on. "That was the worst thing you could have done."

"You would think that it was," Dalila said quietly. "But there's something Meri didn't tell you."

Abdel stole a glance at Meri before addressing Dalila. "What could possibly be worse?"

"I threw the papyrus with the incantation into the water," Dalila confessed. "I wanted to destroy it. The hieroglyphs dissolved, and the papyrus floated away."

"But that didn't destroy the magic," Abdel said.

"I was hoping that it had." Dalila felt her heart drop. She had wanted reassurance, but Abdel had only confirmed her fears.

"You thought you were doing the right thing," Abdel added gently, "but the freed magic is unpredictable. It could become an entity with power of its own."

Dalila didn't like the look that crossed his face. She had an uneasy feeling that there was more he wasn't saying. "Just how dangerous is it?" she asked.

"Worse than you can imagine," he replied.

"You're wrong," Sudi burst out. "It was just a piece of papyrus with writing on it. How could it be anything more? You're acting like it could become something menacing—"

"Like a savage beast or a monster," Abdel said calmly. "That's exactly what I'm telling you."

Sudi rolled her eyes.

If Abdel was offended, it didn't show. His relaxed manner revealed no emotion. "In the beginning of time," he explained, "when the universe was still chaos, powerful forces existed. Those energies didn't disappear after the world was created. Some were benevolent, some not; most were captured, then tamed or charmed by magicians into doing their bidding. The hieroglyphs on the papyrus that you used most likely contained other symbols that kept a primal force imprisoned and obedient to the speaker of the spell. In this case, it had to free Seth and open a path for him to enter our world."

"But after we started the incantation, it felt as if we were hypnotized," Sudi said. "We couldn't stop."

Abdel nodded. "Yes, once the force behind the magic contacted Seth, I'm certain he was able to influence it, and possibly even control it."

"I suppose I should tell you something more," Dalila said.

"More?" Abdel looked surprised.

"I went down to the Tidal Basin this morning," Dalila began. Then, slowly, she recounted everything that had happened, from running away from Mrs. Lavendish to encountering the man who had chased her.

"The man who followed you was Shaitan," Abdel said.

"The devil?" Dalila shuddered. Her uncle had always told her not to speak that name, because even saying it was dangerous. "How can that be?"

"The devil has been Seth's slave since the beginning of time," Abdel explained calmly. "Shaitan can assume human form, but his feet must remain hooves. His footsteps made the clopping you heard. At first, his pupils were rectangular, like those of a goat. That wasn't your imagination. But then he caught himself and made his eyes look human."

"So, what are we supposed to do?" Sudi began nervously playing with a strand of hair.

"Find the magic before Shaitan does," Abdel replied.

"Just like that?" Meri asked. "We don't even know what magic looks like."

"Are we supposed to intuitively know what to do?" Dalila felt frustrated and didn't wait for his reply. She pulled the papyrus that her uncle had given her from her pocket. She hadn't planned on showing it to Abdel, but she wanted to prove to him that the situation was dangerous and that they needed his help.

"My uncle had to leave for Egypt, and he was afraid to leave me alone. He looked at the stars, and, although he wouldn't say, I know he saw something that made him afraid. He gave me this for protection." She handed the papyrus to Abdel.

He glanced down and his shoulders slumped, the movement so slight it might have been her imagination. But when he looked up again, she caught a fleeting glimpse of fear in his eyes. He frowned in order to mask his real emotion and handed the papyrus back to her.

Dalila quickly changed her thoughts about his behavior. She had assumed he was disapproving and angry, but now she wondered if he was afraid. Maybe he had seen something in the stars and, like her uncle, was anticipating something bad.

Abdel cleared his throat. "I must warn you that the next time you see me, I won't know who you are."

"How can you possibly not know us?" Meri started to laugh, but the sadness in Abdel's expression made her stop.

He stood. "I'll leave you now."

"Don't go yet," Sudi pleaded. "We still have a zillion questions."

But Abdel was already pounding up the stairs.

Sudi opened her mouth to say something more, but Dalila placed a hand on her arm and stopped her.

Abdel paused on the landing. "You will soon know all about me, and then I will be able to answer your questions if you still want me to be your mentor."

"That may be too late," Dalila whispered, defeated.

CHAPTER 6

The scents from the restaurants on K Street reminded Dalila that she hadn't eaten. Her stomach growled in response. She rummaged through her purse, found a mint at the bottom, and picked off the lint. She'd never had to worry about eating before. Her tutors and chaperones, as well as her uncle's housekeepers, had always taken care of such details. She had lived a privileged life without appreciating how lucky she had been. But then she looked at Sudi and Meri and remembered the loneliness of her old life.

"What's up with Abdel?" Sudi asked, interrupting Dalila's thoughts.

Meri glanced up at the house. A light came on in the attic window. "What does he mean he won't know us?"

"That doesn't make sense," Sudi said. "Of course he'll know who we are."

"He started acting so strangely after he read the incantation." Dalila looked down at the papyrus her uncle had given her and studied it under the light of the porch lamp.

Sudi and Meri pressed closer, reading the hieroglyphs over her shoulder.

"It's something about praising the sun," Meri said, linking arms with Dalila. "How could that bother anyone?"

"Maybe we don't understand the real meaning," Dalila offered, "because it frightened my uncle when I began reading the words out loud."

"But the papyrus doesn't have anything scary written on it," Sudi insisted. "It's just a tribute to Amun-Re."

"So what now?" Meri started walking down the street.

"I think we should go shopping for something to wear to Sara's party," Sudi said. "I've been looking at this blue, sequined dress."

"It's a costume party," Meri reminded her as they crossed the street. "Sara wants everyone to dress up like an angel."

"So, I'll go as a glamour queen instead," Sudi said.

"That shouldn't be a problem for you," Dalila snickered.

Sudi smiled excitedly, as if an idea had just come to her. "I'll go as a glamour *angel*! You know, like a movie star that died and went to heaven. How cool is that?"

Dalila and Meri stopped on the curb and stared at Sudi.

"What?" Sudi asked defensively. She opened her purse, pulled out a makeup brush and compact, then stared in the mirror and dusted pink color over the apples of her cheeks.

"The devil's chasing us," Dalila snapped. She felt like screaming, but quieted herself. Her burst of anger was only an attempt to hide her real emotions of fear and frustration.

"Jeez, am I supposed to put my life on hold?" Sudi teasingly poked the brush at Dalila and swept the bristles across her nose. "Cheer up, please. You're the one who always gives us courage."

Dalila tried to smile.

"You told us that our minds are like magnets, and whatever we concentrate on we bring into our lives," Sudi went on. "So let's think about something happy. Imagine trying on gorgeous clothes. And there's this new perfume—"

"You're right," Dalila interrupted. "We draw into our lives what we think about most. So let's concentrate on finding the magic."

Sudi threw her makeup into her purse. "That's not the answer I'd hoped to hear."

"We should go down to the Tidal Basin," Meri put in.

"When we're so close to great shopping?" Sudi looked up at the darkening sky. Low-hanging clouds reflected the city lights. "Besides it's freezing; and we don't even know what magic looks like."

"But maybe you'll know it when you see it," Meri said.

"Me?" Sudi asked, her eyes widening. "Why me?"

"For one thing, you're the only one who can change into a bird and fly over the water," Dalila said. "A snake would surely drown."

"And cats hate water." Meri smirked. "So I can't do it."

Sudi looked up. "Birds don't fly in this kind of weather."

"Magic birds do," Dalila assured her.

"All right," Sudi agreed grudgingly.

When they arrived at the Jefferson Memorial, a group of senior citizens were getting off a blue tour bus. Dalila, Meri, and Sudi let the crowd conceal them. Dalila pretended to listen to the guide as she scanned the shadows.

"I don't see anyone who looks like they might belong to the cult," Meri said.

Dalila nodded. "Everything looks safe."

Cautiously, the girls eased away from the tour group and continued walking until they were behind a screen of trees.

Sudi handed Dalila her purse. "All right, here goes," she said with a petulant look. She closed her

eyes, still frowning, and her lips moved, silently reciting an incantation. She flinched and bent forward.

Feathers poked through her clothing and grew from the tips of her fingers. Her arms fluttered into sweeping wings as her lips stretched into a long, slender beak. At the same time, her body shrank, re-forming into a red-and-gold bird with a two-feathered crest, long legs, and an *S*-shaped neck.

The bird pecked Dalila's cheek. "Ouch!" Dalila said.

Then the wings came up and ruffled Meri's hair. "Stop it!" Meri yelled.

After that, the bird let out a fretful cry that sounded more like girlish protest than a bird's squawk as Sudi, in her avian form, ran down to the water. She stretched her wings and caught the air, then flew into the night, a graceful silhouette against the threatening clouds.

Dalila and Meri ran after her, crowding in with the sightseers who were rushing to take pictures of the unusual bird.

Sudi soared higher and higher. But when she banked and turned to glide over the water, she unexpectedly stopped. Her wings flapped oddly, one up, the other down, all elegance gone. With a horrible scream, she plunged toward the ground, becoming a mix of wings and girl legs. Sudi slammed into the tree tops on the other side of the Tidal Basin.

Dalila watched, horror-struck, then started running. Meri sprinted beside her, her footsteps thundering on the concrete walk.

"What happened to her?" Meri asked.

"I don't know." Dalila increased her pace, heartsick. "I just hope she's okay."

Minutes later, they found Sudi, almost buried in a pile of leaves, a girl again, but with feathers poking from her wrists and neck. She groaned.

Dalila and Meri kneeled beside her. "Are you all right?" Dalila asked.

Sudi pressed her fingers against her cheekbones, then tentatively felt the bridge of her nose. "I hope my nose isn't swelling. Are there scratches on my face?"

"Is that all you can think about? How you look?" Meri hugged her. "We're just glad you're alive."

Dalila helped Sudi stand up. "Why did you fall?" she asked after she had assured herself that they didn't need to rush Sudi to the hospital.

"I flew into a web. Or maybe it was a wall? Something invisible caught me," Sudi said, rubbing her elbow. "Whatever it was, it freaked me out and made me lose my concentration."

"The cult must have put a spell over the water so they'd know if we came down here looking for the magic," Meri surmised.

"Or Shaitan did," Dalila added. "Now I know how he was able to find me so quickly when I stirred the water with my wand."

"So, that means the magic must be here," Meri said. "All we have to do is find it first."

"Hide," Sudi said suddenly in a low, harsh voice. She clenched Dalila's hand.

"What?" Dalila and Meri asked at the same time.

Sudi's fingernails dug into Dalila's skin. "We have to hide," she whispered urgently. She staggered back, pulling her friends with her behind a tree trunk.

Dalila followed Sudi's gaze; what she saw made her duck.

Three guys and a girl walked silently along the water's edge, their long winter coats billowing in the night breeze. The four seemed too secretive, slinking forward, trying hard not to make a sound. Their unnatural quietness was frightening. Their faces were hidden in shadow, and the darkness surrounding them made them seem like phantoms floating forward. They didn't carry cameras, maps, or tour brochures, and they weren't looking at the monument.

"They're definitely not tourists," Meri whispered, crouching lower. "Just watching them is giving me the willies. They look like the walking dead."

"They're searching for us," Sudi whispered. "I can feel their energy."

Dalila nodded in agreement. She sensed something evil in the breeze.

"They must be members of the cult," Meri said. "We've never fought members our own age. Do you think they know magic, or do you expect us to fight them with our fists?"

The thought of fighting gave Dalila a queasy feeling. "I don't think I can."

"It doesn't matter," Sudi said. "Either way, we won't win."

"They haven't seen us yet." Dalila eased back, pulling Meri and Sudi with her. Maybe they could quietly leave and avoid a confrontation.

A twig snapped beneath her foot. She froze and felt the tension rising inside Sudi and Meri.

The four stopped. The curious stillness about them reminded Dalila of cats that had caught the scent of prey. She held her breath, trying hard not to move or even blink.

As one, the four turned, their eyes riveted on the screen of trees that hid Dalila and her friends. The tallest stepped off the walkway, his face still covered in shadows. He bent low and crept stealthily toward them.

Dalila's heart beat painfully in her chest. Her ears filled with the rushing sound of her own blood. Then, above that, she heard soft padding, the steady gallop of feet. Fear tightened her stomach muscles. She concentrated, terrified that Shaitan was coming for her.

Instead, a group of joggers, military types with heavy muscles and trim haircuts, came into view.

They ran near the water's edge, their tennis shoes pounding over the walk and crunching twigs and leaves.

The sudden noise confused the four. The one who had been stalking beneath the trees rushed back and joined the other three. Then all four huddled together watching the runners, but, like predators who had been interrupted in their hunt, they seemed to have lost the scent. Slowly, they turned and followed the joggers, moving away from the girls.

When they disappeared behind the overhanging tree limbs, Dalila took in a deep breath. Her muscles began relaxing.

"Let's get out of here," Meri whispered.

Dalila stood up and started to leave.

The cell phone inside Sudi's purse rang.

CHAPTER 7

The cell phone continued playing *Pump It*, the song growing louder and louder. The pack of four turned and came back down the walkway, their steps smooth and quick. They whispered excitedly to one another, then broke apart and furtively slipped beneath the trees, their silhouettes fading into the shadows as they raced toward the place where Dalila, Sudi, and Meri were hiding.

Sudi clung to Dalila, trembling fiercely. "What are we going to do?"

"Go!" Meri shouted, pointing behind Dalila. She took off running. "Hurry!" she shouted.

"Where?" Dalila spun around.

A large orange and white tour bus was parked less than a block away, engine rumbling. The driver had opened the door to let the tourists board.

Dalila gripped Sudi's hand and jerked her arm. Together, they ran at full speed, whipping past skeletal branches. Twigs scraped across Dalila's face and caught in her sleeves. Her shoes squished into sucking mud. She wobbled, almost falling. Sudi stumbled into her. They caught each other, then sprinted on.

"I hate this," Sudi said between rasping breaths. "Why me?" she moaned.

Ahead of them, Meri thrust herself into the line of tourists. She squeezed in front of a large woman who had just started to board the bus and scrambled up the steps.

"Well, I never," the woman complained. When she grabbed on to the hand rail to board the bus again, Dalila and Sudi nudged her out of the way.

"Excuse me, please." Dalila ignored the driver's frown and headed to the back, where Meri stood waiting for them. Dalila fell into the seat and tried to catch her breath. A shadow in the corner of her eye made her turn and look out the window.

The four who had stalked them stood near the streetlamp, no longer bothering to conceal themselves. Their coats caught the wind and blew out behind them. They looked no older than Dalila: high school students. The tallest was darkly handsome, his eyes serious beneath long bangs of coal black hair.

He wasn't smirking or making faces the way the other three were. The girl waved, then blew a kiss, striking a Hollywood pose, before she fell against the guy next to her. They both laughed and pointed at Dalila.

"They think it's funny that we're scared," Meri said, her voice trembling.

"I guess they were guarding the water so we wouldn't get to the magic first," Dalila said. Her chest felt heavy with defeat.

"Whatever." Sudi took her purse from Dalila and pulled out her cell phone. "Anyone who

wants to bring chaos into the world is a total loser."
She formed her fingers into an *L* and flashed it
at the window, then yelled, "Zack, you're such a
freak."

In response, the tallest one shrugged. Sudi's
outrage made the group laugh even harder.

"You know him?" Dalila stared back at the
guy.

Sudi opened her cell phone. "He goes to my
school," she replied, not looking up.

"What are you doing?" Meri asked as she
picked red bird feathers from Sudi's hair.

"I'm checking to see who called." Sudi scrolled
down, concentrating on the screen. "Isn't it obvious?"

"I can't believe you're worried about missing a
call," Meri said.

Sudi turned sharply and held up her phone for
Meri and Dalila to read.

The caller ID displayed the name Zack.

"It was him," Sudi whispered in a thin voice.
Her eyes brimmed with tears. "If Zack is a member
of the cult, then how many other kids at my school
are?" She shook her head. "I just want it to all

go away so I can go back to my life the way it was."

Sudi's phone rang again, startling her. It fell from her hands and skipped down the aisle until it hit a man's foot and stopped. Then, with trembling hands, she picked it up and read the screen. Her shoulders relaxed. "It's Sara!" she shouted and answered the phone. "Hey!"

Meri leaned against Dalila. "It isn't fair," she whispered. "We're expected to do so much, but no one is telling us how. What would have happened if they had caught us?" Meri asked. "Do you think they would have hurt us?"

"I don't know," Dalila answered and looked back out the window. The girl had stopped laughing. Her dead gaze petrified Dalila.

Finally, the bus pulled away from the curb. Dalila leaned back and closed her eyes as they sped down Constitution Avenue.

Sudi spoke into her phone, and when she snapped it closed, she twisted in her seat until she was facing Dalila and Meri again. "Sara's setting up for her Sweet Sixteen tomorrow night, and Michelle is there, trying to make the party all about her. I know you're both really tired, but please don't say no. We have to help Sara." She gave them a pleading look.

Dalila was bruised, cut, and filthy, and on top of that she felt drained and hungry. She wanted to go home, but she also knew how much helping Sara meant to Sudi.

Meri nodded.

"Sure," Dalila agreed, trying to smile.

"Besides, Carter might be there," Sudi added, handing Dalila her makeup bag, "and I know you want to see him."

Dalila glanced down at her pant legs and wondered what Carter would think when he saw her splattered with mud again.

By the time the bus had stopped in front of the Marriott Courtyard, Sudi, Meri, and Dalila had combed one another's hair and picked the leaves from their clothing.

Sudi jumped up, putting more gloss on her lips. "We can walk from here."

Dalila and Meri followed her off the bus, and soon they were passing the International Spy Museum and heading down F Street. A white tent and generators had already been set up at the west entrance of the National Building Museum in preparation for Sara's party. The girls entered in the front and took off their muddy shoes before going through the second set of doors.

The Great Hall had been decorated with Sara's artwork. Angels with fanciful wings dangled from the skylight between differing lengths of gauzy material. The shiny cloth swirled with each movement of air, giving the illusion that the angels were flying.

"It's so beautiful," Dalila whispered, trying to take in everything at once. A few angels held long trumpets, others appeared to be singing, while some held their hands together in prayers.

"Wow!" Sudi exclaimed, gazing up. She stepped between two pieces of gossamer fabric that hung down to the floor.

"It looks like heaven," Meri said breathlessly, her eyes wide.

A giant plasma screen hung behind the stage, looking out of place among the sparkling angels' wings.

Brian and Scott sat slouched in folding chairs

near the water fountain, appearing bored, but when they saw Dalila, Sudi, and Meri, their eyes brightened. They immediately came over to greet the girls.

After everyone said hello, Dalila asked timidly, "Why isn't Carter with you?"

"He told us that he had to go away for a few days," Scott replied. "Didn't he say anything to you?"

Dalila's stomach dropped. She shook her head. "Did he say why?"

Michelle pushed in front of Scott before he could answer. She was wearing a black bodysuit and ropes of jangling chains. She twirled in front of Sudi and Dalila.

"What do you think?" she asked. "Gorgeous, right? My dad bought it for me in Paris." Without waiting for an answer, she linked arms with Sudi and Dalila, purposely ignoring Meri. "I need your help," she said.

"Don't listen to her," someone cried from the east court. Sara ran toward them, maneuvering around the billowing fabric.

Michelle continued in a low voice, paying no attention to Sara. "We need to help Sara. She's planning this silly costume party, but it's not too late to save her from a real social blunder. I mean, she can't expect people to dress up like angels. That's so . . ." Michelle rolled her eyes in frustration. "Why can't I think of a word to describe how horrible this situation truly is?" Then her face brightened. "*Vraiment pas* cool," she said finally, looking proud of herself.

"But that's what I want," Sara interjected. Her mascara was smudged, her eyes red. "Angels!"

"Who ever heard of that for your Sweet Sixteen?" Michelle went on. "It's so démodé, and Sara's a rising star. I mean, just look at the decorations she's put up. She's an incredible artist, and she's worked on the angels for years."

"Precisely!" Sara shouted. "That's why I don't want my night ruined."

Michelle disregarded Sara's comment and continued, "We don't want her to fall in popularity just because she doesn't know how to plan a party. Let's help her."

"And what did you have in mind?" Sudi asked.

"Don't." Sara looked ready to faint.

"I'll show you." Michelle jumped up on the stage.

Scott shook his head. "I don't think I want to hear this again."

"I know I don't," Sara said unhappily.

Dalila felt a hand on her waist, and fingers caressed her hip. She swung around, expecting to see Carter, but Brian was smiling down at her. She wriggled free.

"We're going over to The Jackal to go dancing," he said. "Want to come along?"

"No," she replied. The Jackal was the most popular teen club in the District, owned and operated by the cult.

"Come on," Brian said, pressing closer.

Dalila knew he was getting ready to bully her into going out with him.

"Get real, Brian," Sudi said, stepping between them. "Why would she want to go out with you?"

Brian glared at Sudi. "Can't you just get over me?"

"I am *so* over you, Brian," Sudi countered angrily. "And where's Dominique? Are you trying to do to her what you did to me?"

"You and I were through way before I started seeing Dominique," Brian argued.

"Right," Sudi said sarcastically. Dalila knew Sudi's breakup with Brian had been bad, but she had never told Dalila what had happened between them.

A high-pitched, unpleasant voice interrupted their squabble, and suddenly everyone was drawn toward the stage by Michelle's outrageous performance. She thrust her hands stiffly about, her cadence wrong, and tried rapidly to recite a birthday tribute to Sara. Dalila stared in disbelief.

"You've got to stop her," Sara said mournfully. "I've tried already."

"Why does she think she's so talented?" Brian asked.

"Because you encourage her, when the rest of us are trying to tell her the truth," Scott said. "You think it's funny when she makes a fool out of herself."

Brian smiled in an irritatingly smug way. "Oh, yeah, that's right."

"Then why do you pretend to be her friend?" Sudi asked crossly.

Brian shrugged. "Because Michelle's a joke."

"I can't let her ruin my party." Sara moaned. But she looked too overwhelmed to do anything about it. "What makes her think she has the right?"

"Because she's Michelle," Brian and Scott said. Brian laughed loudly, but Scott just shook his head.

Dalila didn't particularly like Michelle, but she wasn't going to let her embarrass herself. She walked over to the stage. "Stop!"

"You didn't let me finish," Michelle whined. "I thought this would be so much better than singing Happy Birthday to Sara in the traditional way, but she doesn't like it."

"I wonder why," Meri said scornfully.

Michelle jumped off the stage. "After I do my rap, I'm going to go around the room with my cameraman and ask everyone to wish Sara Happy B-day." She pointed to the screen. "Our images will be projected there for everyone to see."

"Stop her," Sara said. "I want my angels to be the center of attention, but she won't listen to me."

"But it's your face, not Sara's, that everyone will see," Meri said, trying to persuade Michelle that her idea was wrong.

"So?" Michelle looked genuinely puzzled.

"It's Sara's party," Sudi explained.

"I'm doing all this for Sara," Michelle replied. "I want her Sweet Sixteen to be perfect."

Then Dalila saw a woman dressed in jeans sitting on the floor and studying papers on a clipboard. The woman kept brushing back the curls that tumbled over her shoulders into her face.

"She has to be the party planner." Dalila straightened her back and strode over to her, Meri following quickly behind her.

The woman looked harried and upset. One earring was missing, and she was biting her fingernails.

"I assume you're in charge of the party." Dalila sat down beside her.

The woman nodded without looking up.

"I don't understand why you're allowing Michelle to change a party that has already been planned," Dalila said.

The woman glanced at Dalila and blinked. "Who are you?" she asked.

"Does that matter?" Dalila asked. "Why are you allowing Michelle to do anything she wants?"

The party planner looked nervous. "Michelle's dad is our biggest client. My boss said to let Michelle perform." She cringed. "But she's awful."

"Maybe you should tell her father that Michelle is only embarrassing herself," Dalila suggested.

The woman stared at Dalila. "Tell him that his perfect daughter isn't perfect?" She snorted. "I'd lose my job."

Unfazed, Dalila went on, "When he hears that you allowed her to make a fool of herself, I doubt that he'll trust you enough to hire you again. That could definitely cost you your job."

"And who's going to tell him?" the woman asked.

Dalila caught Meri's hand and pulled her down on the floor beside her. "You know Meri Stark, don't you? Her picture is always in the paper."

A flash of recognition passed through the woman's eyes. She smiled brightly. "Senator Stark's daughter, of course," she said in an artificial tone as she extended her hand.

Meri shook it. "Michelle's father is the fund-raiser for my mother's presidential campaign."

Sudi sat down on the floor next to them. "And Michelle and Meri are practically like sisters." She grinned, enjoying her lie.

"I'd hate to see people laugh at Michelle," Meri added, trying to look sincere.

"You're right." The woman got up and walked over to Michelle. "I've made a decision."

"I knew you'd love my piece," Michelle said, obviously anticipating compliments.

"It's not your party," the woman said firmly. "You can't change the plans that Sara has already made."

Thank you, Sara mouthed to Dalila, Sudi, and Meri.

Michelle looked stunned. Her mouth dropped open; then she recovered, and a look of calm determination filled her eyes. "We'll see about that."

CHAPTER 8

That night, when Dalila arrived home, she was surprised to find the house dark. No one was waiting up for her. She went inside, expecting to smell dinner left warming for her, but instead she breathed in the bitter scent of ashes smoldering in the fireplace. A faint clattering came from her uncle's study.

She took off her shoes and socks and crept barefoot down the hall. Timidly, she tapped on the door of the study, not sure if she should disturb him. The clicking of keys continued without a pause. She imagined her uncle sitting in front of his computer screen frantically typing across the keyboard, trying to take care of some last-minute details before his trip. He probably hadn't even heard her knock.

Disappointed, she gave up, went into the kitchen, and made a cup of tea. She wondered why no one had missed her. Had they even worried when she didn't show up for dinner? She had always been so meekly obedient. Maybe they had assumed she was sulking after her uncle's scolding and they had decided to ignore her sullen mood, not realizing that she wasn't hiding in the house, lost in a book, but gone.

As she stepped out of the kitchen and started up the stairs, her throat tightened. Anger was brewing inside her, and she wasn't sure why. She was angry at Michelle, of course, for being so obnoxious, but Michelle was the least of her worries. She felt miffed at Carter for leaving without telling her, but mostly she was worried that her uncle had upset him.

Then, too, she was furious with Abdel. She

wanted to scream at him. He expected her to retrieve the magic before Shaitan found it, but he wouldn't tell her how, and now she suspected it was too late. She felt certain Shaitan had the magic, but how was she going to steal it back without help from Abdel?

She entered her room and glanced at the note that Mrs. Lavendish had propped up against a book. It gave Dalila their schedule for the next day. Annoyed, she crumpled the paper and tossed it aside.

She had always been docile and eagerly ready to follow instructions. But that was before, back when she had thought she was being reared to marry a prince, not fight demons. She felt betrayed, and the very source of her betrayal was the one person she had trusted the most: her uncle. She picked up the figurine of the goddess Isis that he had given her when she was eight and threw it across the room. The shattering of the porcelain gave her only a moment's satisfaction. Immediately, she wished she hadn't broken her treasured statue.

Her door opened without warning, and her uncle peeked into her room. He looked even more worn than when she had seen him earlier; the skin around his eyes was dark. "Do we need to have a talk, Dalila?" he asked.

She looked down at her hands, ashamed, and shook her head, hating the tears that betrayed her. "Why didn't you tell me before?"

He sat beside her on the edge of the bed and took her hand, patting it gently as he had always done when he was trying to calm her. "I couldn't tell a little girl of seven who had just lost her parents that she was someday going to stand against ancient gods and fight evil. Even if I had told you when you were ten, would you have believed me? At best you would have thought I was joking. More likely you would have assumed I'd lost my mind."

Dalila had to admit that what he said was true, although she refused to nod and agree with him. "Have you always known what I was?" she asked.

"Since your birth I've known," he said.

She glanced at her uncle, wondering how he knew so much, but the question didn't form on her lips. She wasn't ready for that answer yet.

"God in His mercy doesn't show us the

future," her uncle explained. "Would any of us have the courage to go on if we could see what would happen in the days ahead?" He didn't wait for her to answer but continued, "Even if you had believed me, it would have been wrong to tell you. Fear of the future would have consumed you. You wouldn't have been able to concentrate and learn what you needed to know."

Dalila wondered if that were true. "So you let me believe I was to marry a prince."

"You were always a princess," he teased, trying to pull her out of her bad mood. "You still deserve a prince, but for now you must focus on all that I taught you and regain your confidence."

She looked up at him. "How do you know what I'm feeling?"

"I can see your self-doubt. Your boldness is gone." He touched the hair near her temple. "You're even afraid to flaunt your birthmark."

"But it marks me . . ." She couldn't bring herself to say *for death*. Just the same, her stomach pinched. She took in a deep breath. "Abdel doesn't tell us what to do," she grumbled, needing her uncle's comfort. "He doesn't give us instruction."

"Complaining never helps," her uncle cautioned. "You're a wise young woman, Dalila. I have every confidence in you."

She sighed. "I wish I felt the same way."

Her uncle kissed her forehead, then pulled himself up, bracing his hands on his knees. His slow movement worried her. His first step came as a stumble. She jumped up, trying to steady him, and walked with him as far as her bedroom door.

"Come say good-bye to me when you leave," she whispered. He looked old and ill. Suddenly, she was afraid this might be the last time she would see him. "Promise. Even if I'm asleep, wake me."

"I promise," he said, even though she doubted that he would. He never had before.

"I'm serious," she said.

He nodded. His slow steps continued down the hallway. Old age had come to him quickly, and yet he was only fifty. She sensed that stress was wearing him down, and immediately she felt guilty.

After a long shower, she got ready for bed. By the time she crawled under the covers, her eyes were beginning to close on their own. She rolled over, exhausted, and glanced out her window. She thought she saw someone standing in the tree, balanced on a branch, watching her. A breeze stirred the leaves, and the figure became a tangle of tree limbs. She smiled to herself, remembering the way her wild imaginings had scared her as a child.

Sleep had already taken Dalila when the window opened.

CHAPTER 9

Hours later, Dalila awakened. Someone was calling her name. She swung her legs off the bed and drowsily pulled on her quilted robe. A sharp, cold wind raced across her face. Puzzled and awake now, she realized her window was open. She closed it, then hurried into the hallway, seeking warmth. The furnace vents rattled, blowing hot air into the house, but the heat was immediately whisked away by an icy draft. She shivered and folded her arms across her chest.

On the landing, she saw that the front door was open. Her uncle was most likely waiting for her outside, to say good-bye.

She rushed down the stairs and onto the front walk, but he wasn't there.

Frost covered the lawn. The frozen grass gleamed under the moon's glow and crunched beneath her feet. She stepped outside, into a world of lustrous white, and, ignoring the ache that traveled up her bones from the freezing ground, she continued to stare at the fairy-tale night. When a breeze stirred the trees overhead, tiny ice stars shimmered and fell across her upturned face.

From the corner of her eye, she caught a peculiar orange glow. She looked back at the house to find the source and her breath caught. A fire burned behind the windows in her uncle's study.

She dashed back into the house, terrified that he had fallen asleep while smoking his pipe. She raced down the hallway, screaming his name, and didn't understand why her ruckus didn't awaken Mrs. Lavendish or the housekeeper.

Flames crackled and hissed from behind his door. She prayed he hadn't locked it. The knob turned. She threw herself into the room. Flames shot up to the ceiling, the heat unbearable. She staggered back, unable at first to understand what she saw.

The goddess Isis stood behind the fire

"I've been calling your name." Isis gazed at Dalila through the blaze. "I need to speak with you."

"What is it?" Dalila held her hand up to shield her eyes from the brightness and the blistering temperature. "Why did you set fire to my uncle's office? Are you angry with him?"

"Not him." Isis studied the flames like someone staring into a crystal ball. "My scrying glass told me that you would betray me. I didn't believe what it foretold. So I decided to use pyromancy to gaze into the future. The flames tell me the same."

"That's impossible," Dalila said. Sparks shot into the air and spiraled down, encircling Dalila. "I've done nothing wrong."

Isis shook her head with an expression of sad disappointment. "I hold the greatest secrets of the universe, and I gave that magic to you. Would you betray me after I have given you so much?"

"No," Dalila protested. "Never."

"Yet I foresee in the flames that you will put terrible magic into an incantation to free the god Seth, my eternal enemy, from the prison in which I cast him." Tears ran down the cheeks of the goddess and doused the blaze. Without the fire, the room became cold and silent. The only light came from the nimbus that encircled Isis.

"Seth is my enemy." Dalila coughed and fanned her face with her hands, waving away the smoke.

"I can't see what will become of you, Dalila, because unfamiliar magic is blocking me." Isis looked bewildered. "I am the queen of magic. The mightiest of the gods seek my help, so how can that be?"

"Maybe Shaitan . . ." Dalila began but stopped when Isis scowled.

"I am the one who deceived our great father Amun-Re and tricked him into giving me his secret name so that my power would be greater than all." Isis frowned petulantly. "Are you telling me that Shaitan has stronger magic than mine?"

"Not stronger," Dalila stammered. "But I'm afraid he has the magic I released." She started to tell Isis everything that had happened when suddenly the telephone rang.

The sound startled Isis. She vanished.

Dalila switched on the light and wondered how something as ordinary as the ringing of a telephone could have frightened Isis. She stared at the desk where the fire had been and ran her fingers along the cool, smooth edge. There was no trace of ash or charring, even though smoke still hung thickly in the room.

The phone continued ringing. Dalila never answered her uncle's private line. She stepped toward the hallway.

The answering machine clicked on, and a voice came through the speaker: *I know you're there, Dalila. Pick up the receiver so that you can talk to me.*

Stunned, Dalila hurried back and reached for the phone, then stopped, certain Shaitan was the person on the other end.

He seemed to sense her hesitation.

If I can block the goddess Isis from using her magic, the voice continued, *then maybe you should consider listening to what I have to offer you.*

But instead of answering the phone, Dalila

bolted from the room. She could hear the voice on the machine laughing at her panic.

Her breath was coming in gasps by the time she reached the top of the stairs. She went first to her uncle's room. His bed was made, his suitcases gone. Frantic, she stumbled back down the hall to Mrs. Lavendish's door. Her hand stopped in midair, poised to knock, and then she leaned her forehead against the wood and let out a sigh. Even if she could make Mrs. Lavendish believe her, what could Mrs. Lavendish do against Shaitan?

Defeated, she went back to her room, closed the drapes, and crawled back into bed. She tried to remember everything her uncle had taught her about the old ways. He had given her spells when she was a child to protect her from nightmares and the monsters she imagined hiding under her bed. She had assumed that it had only been his way of comforting her. Now she wondered.

The words she had spoken as a child came unpracticed and stuttering from her lips: *"Aha-a sexem a xesef-a madret-d."* She repeated the incantation in English: "I rise up. I gain power over and repulse the evil which is against me."

A dim orange glow lit her room, becoming brighter until she was unable to see past her blankets. The magic settled over her. The light faded, but not the comfort. She was safe, at least for this night.

CHAPTER 10

The following morning, Dalila woke up to the cinnamon-and-cloves scent of her favorite tea. The housekeeper had brought in her breakfast and set it on the table in the alcove by the bay window. The room was blessedly warm, and Dalila didn't bother with her robe. As she poured her tea, she made a decision to visit Abdel, alone this time, and tell him everything that had happened the previous night.

But first she needed to memorize the incantation

that her uncle had given her. She sipped her tea and diligently studied the hieroglyphs.

As she began to butter a croissant, a loud crash startled her. The noise was immediately followed by a thud.

Shadows brushed back and forth in the bar of light beneath her door. She waited, wondering why Mrs. Lavendish or the housekeeper hadn't knocked.

Urgent, excited whispers—two voices at least, and definitely not those of Mrs. Lavendish and the housekeeper—came from the hallway.

Then, hoof beats clattered across the hardwood floor.

Adrenaline shot through Dalila. She grabbed the incantation, intending to use it, but as she unrolled the papyrus, Shaitan burst into the room, his gaze deadlier than before. The papyrus fell from her hand and floated down to the floor.

A moment later, Zack and one of the other guys who had chased her at the Tidal Basin followed Shaitan into her room.

"Good morning, Dalila," Shaitan said.

Without thinking, she took the teapot and threw it at him. It hit his forehead and shattered, spilling scalding tea over him. He screamed, not in pain but in rage, as he lunged forward and seized her.

She struggled in his arms, trying to remember the spell her uncle had given her.

"Stop moving, Dalila," Shaitan ordered. "We only need to talk. You'll consider me your friend once you hear what I have to offer you. I can give you the world."

"I don't want it," she answered. She squirmed, and, inch by inch, her struggling forced him to move closer to her dresser.

Exasperated, he lifted his hand up in a curious curl. With a jolt of new fear, she realized he was going to cast a spell on her to make her obedient. When his mouth opened to speak, she swung her elbow back with all her power. The blow didn't hurt him, but the surprise of it was enough to keep him from speaking.

Zack and his friend hooted, making fun of her futile attempt to save herself. Shaitan snarled at them. They fell silent. Even so, their grins didn't fade.

While he was focused on them, Dalila had

eased him even closer to her dresser. She could touch it now. Her fingers scrabbled over the surface, searching for anything she could use as a weapon. She grasped a bottle of perfume and sprayed. As the fragrance hit Shaitan's skin, the scent changed into something foul. Holding her breath, Dalila tried again.

Success! This time she got his eyes. He cried out and cursed. He didn't let her go, but his grip loosened enough that she was able to pull free. She sprinted past Zack and his friend. Their shocked expressions made her scream a triumphant "*Ha-ha!*"

When she reached the stairs, a fourth person caught her from behind and, holding her tight, swung her down the hallway. Dalila was thrown to the floor in her uncle's bedroom. The door slammed, and a lock clicked. She lay sprawled on the carpet, the taste of blood filling her mouth.

CHAPTER 11

A hand touched Dalila's cheek, stroking it gently. She glanced up, surprised to see Mrs. Lavendish leaning over her, holding a gun tightly at her side. Her face was bruised, her left eye swelling, but she smiled encouragingly. "I'm sorry I had to be so rough with you, but I needed to get you away from the kidnappers."

"Is that what you think they are?" Dalila asked, standing up.

"Lock the door after I go out," Mrs. Lavendish said, ignoring her question. "And call nine-one-one."

"You can't fight them." Dalila tried to stop Mrs. Lavendish, but she had already slipped back out into the hallway.

Something crashed against the wall, and the gun fired.

The sound shocked Dalila, but the silence that followed was worse.

"Mrs. Lavendish?" Dalila called.

"Everything's under control," Mrs. Lavendish called back, her voice calm and resolute.

But Dalila knew she couldn't leave Mrs. Lavendish there alone against Shaitan. Warily, she opened the door, her nerves thrumming.

Mrs. Lavendish stood nearby, back pressed against the wall, the gun still in her hands, the barrel pointed at Shaitan. A shattered vase lay at her feet. Maybe one of the guys had thrown it at her.

Dalila joined her.

"Get back in the room!" Mrs. Lavendish ordered. Her eyes never left Shaitan; she was apparently so intent on targeting him that she didn't notice the hooves poking out from the bottom of his pant legs.

The two guys who had accompanied Shaitan now cowered in the stairwell. They peeked out, their faces pale with fear.

Shaitan stood in front of them, not eight feet from Dalila.

"I shot him at point-blank range," Mrs. Lavendish said when Dalila didn't leave.

Dalila understood at once. "The bullets passed through him."

"No," Mrs. Lavendish said, without moving her head. "I must have missed."

"Really?" Shaitan walked straight toward Mrs. Lavendish. He cocked his head, his smile taunting her.

"Stay back," she warned.

He kept coming, and she fired again.

The deafening explosion resounded through the hallway. Dalila's ears were still aching from the blast when Shaitan tore the gun from Mrs. Lavendish and tossed it over the railing. He leaned threateningly close.

Dalila could smell the sour odor of his breath. She tried to remember the spell she had cast around herself the night before for protection.

"Run, Dalila!" Mrs. Lavendish yelled.

Shaitan's hand came up. Mrs. Lavendish braced her back against the wall, steeling herself for his attack.

At the same moment, Dalila remembered the incantation. *"Aha-a sexem a xesef-a madret-d."* An orange glow filled the air. Dalila swept her hand around it and sent it over to Mrs. Lavendish.

The light formed a cocoon around the woman. She looked up, surprised. Then her eyelids fluttered. Her head lolled forward, and she slid down the wall until she was sitting limply in a faint, her arms and legs splayed out in front of her.

Shaitan jerked his hand back. His fingers were blistered where the magic had scalded his skin. His mouth stretched into a horrible smile. He lifted his head and sniffed something in the air.

"The scent of your terror delights me, Dalila." He stood still, discerning something more. "I can feel your heart racing, and it gives me such joy. You really should have spoken to me last night. A simple conversation could have saved us so much time. But you'll listen to me now."

Dalila inched away from him. Then, without warning, she swung around and dashed into her bedroom. She slammed the door and frantically picked up the papyrus.

Instinctively facing the morning sun, she began reading the praises to Amun-Re. "Glorious creator, shining master of life, king of the earth, strong and mighty giver of life, beyond all the gods, fast riding across the skies, thou—"

The door opened, and Shaitan leaped across the threshold, intent on stopping her.

She concentrated on the hieroglyphs, her anxiety rising as she loudly intoned her tribute. Her voice trembled. The papyrus fluttered.

As Shaitan reached for her, she spoke the words: "I have walked on thy rays as a ramp under my feet."

Without warning, the sunlight became so radiant it pained her to look at it.

Shaitan yelled and shielded his eyes with his hands.

The shafts of light pulled together, forming a

narrow path that curved upward. Dalila's heart beat wildly as she realized it was a bridge. She didn't know where it would take her, but at the moment she didn't care.

With a burst of adrenaline, she raced forward, her feet pounding over the glistening sun-stones. She glanced over her shoulder. The bridge seemed to vanish behind her as she stepped over it. That gave her hope. She increased her speed, pumping hard.

Loud clopping told her that Shaitan had followed her on to the bridge. His rasping breath sounded closer. Without warning, his hand shot out and caught her shoulder. Then, with a cry of despair, she lost her balance and fell, skidding forward. Whimpering, she surrendered and waited for him to pounce on her.

Instead, he yelled, then cursed in anger.

She rolled over. The bridge had disappeared beneath his hooves. He was falling back into the darkness beneath him, but as he tumbled his hand came up, and his fingers marked the air, drawing out a spell. A lightning bolt shot up and struck the bridge. The bricks joggled and shook.

Dalila slipped backward, slowly at first, then faster. She dug her fingers into the seams between the bricks, but couldn't stop her slide. She slid off the opposite side of the bridge.

CHAPTER 12

D alila's feet hit something solid. She swung her arms out for balance and hurriedly looked around. She had landed on a dock made of granite. Waves from a large river lapped against the stone. Across the water, boats made from bundled reeds bobbed in the current. A royal barge moored near them was adorned with gold, its sides inlaid with precious stones. The sacred eye of Horus decorated the prow. Dalila had only seen an artist's rendition of such a boat before.

"This can't be," Dalila breathed in shocked surprise. Everything around her indicated that she had escaped into the past. She turned and gazed at the massive temples, certain she was in Egypt, but in what century?

The haunting voice of a Lector priest began reciting spells. Someone important had died, and the mummified body was ready to be sealed in its tomb. Dalila had read the text, but her uncle had told her that no one knew how the ancient words were spoken in liturgy. Now she listened, awestruck, to the rise and fall of the mournful chant.

But her fascination lasted only a moment. She didn't have an incantation for returning home. This wasn't like being trapped in a cellar. She was lost in time, with no way to span the years and go back to the twenty-first century.

She tried to force herself to remain calm and to concentrate. Her uncle would never have abandoned her here. The spell must work both ways. She looked around her, hoping the incantation had fallen nearby, but then she remembered with horrible clarity that she had dropped it before she ran over the bridge.

A more immediate danger tore her from her worries. A shadow within a distant papyrus swamp made the leafy heads bend and sway. It entered the river. Something large glided under the water, swimming rapidly toward Dalila. Crocodiles and hippopotamuses had lived along the Nile in ancient times. She had heard her uncle talk with other archaeologists, who had surmised that people were probably the animals' favorite prey.

The shadow picked up speed and rammed the dock. The shock wave shuddered though Dalila and made her stumble back. She teetered on the edge before splashing into the water on the other side of the dock, away from the shadowy predator.

Her head surfaced. She flailed around, but her struggle was useless: she had never learned how to swim. Something stirred the water nearby—something with powerful jaws and teeth that could rend her flesh to shreds.

She started to go under again, but this time her hand hit stone. Pain raced up her arm, and she received it with joy. She clutched the edge of a block of granite, found a foothold, and managed to climb out. She rolled onto the dock as a crocodile surged up, its gaping mouth inches from her face. She cried out as the jaws snapped closed.

A tail shot into the air, then splashed down into the water. The wave washed over her. She scrambled away on her hands and knees. When she was safely behind a wall barrier, she stood up, still woozy from the encounter. Her uncle and his friends had been right. The creature had learned how to become a dangerous and efficient predator.

Terror and despair were working on her. She sniffled, then pressed both hands over her eyes, forcing back her tears. If she was going to survive, she needed to find a safe place where she could rest and regain her strength. She glanced at the temples along the western banks. Ritual offerings of food would have been left out for the gods inside.

In spite of her fear, her mouth began watering as she thought about the taste of pomegranates and figs. She would eat, then curl behind a pillar and sleep. When her thinking was clear again, she would decide what to do, but if she tried to consider her situation now, panic would consume her.

A jackal howled. She hurried away from its

hypnotic cries and ran down a path lined with sphinxes toward the first temple.

The flames of the fire torches and oil-burning lamps jerked and flapped, making shadows jump around her as she passed through the giant pylons. She eased inside and crept toward the inner sanctuary, anxious to find the statue of the god and the food left as an offering for it.

She slowed her steps. Someone was moving nearby, his bare feet padding on the floor. Cautiously, she stepped around a gigantic column and stopped, unable to believe what she saw.

Carter stood in front of the shrine, bare-chested and dressed in the kilt of nobility.

He looked up, and his eyes widened. "Dalila?"

CHAPTER 13

Dalila spun around. Statues of jackals surrounded her. With shock, she realized she was inside a temple dedicated to Anubis.

"Neb-ta-djeser, lord of the sacred land," she whispered.

The jackal-headed god had once had power over evildoers and had been the Egyptian funerary god until Osiris supplanted him. But some of the priests who served Anubis had refused to surrender their power, and they eventually became the leaders of the cult that Dalila fought today. She looked around, certain she was in one of the desecrated temples used for the worship of Seth.

"Dalila?" Carter stepped toward her, rousing her from her thoughts.

His smile confused her. He obviously wasn't ashamed or embarrassed; he seemed relaxed and happy to see her. Maybe he didn't know that the cult was her enemy. She tried to hold on to that belief. Perhaps he hadn't understood that he was devoting his life to evil. But reason told her that if he was here in the past, then the cult leaders had entrusted him with their magic. They wouldn't have given it to him unless he had already proven his loyalty.

"I hate you," she said breathlessly.

He stopped, taken aback. "What?"

She dug her fingernails into her palms and clenched her jaw. When she had composed herself, she continued, "It wasn't a coincidence that you found me down at the Tidal Basin. You knew I'd be there, because you're a member of the cult. That's why you weren't shocked to see me covered with mud and shivering, because you . . ." She coughed. Anger was choking her.

"I knew you had transformed into a cobra to escape Shaitan." Carter finished for her. "I was impressed that you were able to fool him."

She hated the way her chin quivered, betraying the depth of her emotions. "My uncle wasn't upset because you have a bad reputation, was he?"

"No. He sensed my magic the first time you introduced me to him," Carter explained.

"Magic," she murmured. "You have powers, abilities, and yet I never knew." She reeled, suddenly seeing so many things in a new way. "That's why my wand reacted to your touch. It was trying to warn me that you're my enemy. I can't believe how easily you deceived me. Did you make me fall in love with you, too? Are my feelings for you only a spell you cast over me?"

"Your feelings are your own," he reassured her.

Then another thought pushed all others away. "But if you're a member of the cult, why did you go down to the Tidal Basin?" she asked.

"To rescue you," he said simply.

"Rescue me," she repeated. Her emotions had

jumped from hate and anger to love with rampaging speed. She wanted to swoon into his arms. "You were going to save me from Shaitan."

"Yes." He took her in his arms, and she rested her cheek against his bare chest. His warmth soothed her. He wasn't her enemy. He had intended to rescue her.

"If I'd known you were the Enchantress," he chuckled, "I wouldn't have had to worry so much." He leaned down to kiss her, but she pulled away from him.

"Enchantress? What does that mean?" She didn't like the way his smile had twisted rapidly into a frown.

"If you don't know, then why are you here?" He looked genuinely puzzled.

She could hear the stress in his voice, even though he was trying hard to hide his alarm.

"I had to escape," she began. She told him about the incantation that her uncle had given her, and what had happened. "Shaitan was trying to capture me," she explained, "so I used the spell. A bridge formed. I ran over it, and it brought me here."

But then something occurred to her. "No, that's not quite true. Shaitan worked some kind of magic as he was falling into the darkness. A lightning bolt struck the bridge, and maybe that sent me off course."

"You're not supposed to be here," Carter said. "And I won't let Shaitan use you against your will."

"What does that mean?" she asked in a shaky voice, certain she didn't want to hear the answer.

The rattling of sistrums filled the air, a normal sound inside a temple, yet Carter stiffened, appearing alarmed.

"What is it?" Dalila asked.

Without answering, he took her hand and guided her behind a pillar.

The metallic clatter grew louder, and then the rhythmic beat of clappers joined in.

Moments later, blue smoke wreathed itself around them. The heavy, cloying aroma filled the air and made it difficult to breathe. Dalila felt dizzy.

Carter stared, unblinking, at the procession that was coming toward them.

A flame sputtered from one of the torches. Embers snapped in the air. Carter jumped, startled by the sound. He looked into the shadows behind him. His eyes flicked back and forth.

"You're scaring me," Dalila whispered. "What's wrong? Is Shaitan here?"

His scowl silenced her; he looked out again at the procession.

Her heart began to race. She wondered what being the Enchantress meant. Carter hadn't appeared troubled when he saw her. In fact, he had seemed pleased. He had only become concerned when he realized that she didn't know what being the Enchantress meant. Why had that upset him? she wondered. She pressed against him and followed his gaze.

A line of priests marched solemnly toward them. They were bare-chested and had shaved their body and facial hair. The first one carried the *imy-ut*: a headless black animal pelt that hung from the end of a pole.

The next priest, much shorter than the first, held a bowl in the crook of his arm. He dipped his fingers into it and sprinkled water over the corridor—a ritual cleansing of the sanctuary.

Following him came two men carrying a large gold vessel between them. A silver mist spilled over the sides, seeping out and back in, in a sinuous dance. It curled up, rising high, then paused, luminous, seeming to focus its attention on Dalila. She could feel it watching her. She ducked back, afraid, unable understand why the strange vapor should make her feel so uneasy.

"What are they carrying?" she whispered.

Carter glanced down at her. "Magic. Don't you even know that? I thought you were a Descendant."

She started to blame Abdel, but instead stopped and gazed back at the mist.

Instinctively, she knew it was the same magic that she had unwittingly freed when she threw the papyrus into the Tidal Basin. She had to figure out a way to steal it back, but how? The vessel in which it was carried looked too heavy for her to lift, and she didn't think she could just pick up the mist and lug it away, either. She sensed that it would fight her, but there was something more: she was afraid of it. She didn't want to touch it.

"Come on." Carter led her to a dark corner. "Stay here until I get back."

"Can't I go with you?" She didn't want to be left by herself, and at the same time, she wasn't sure she could trust Carter.

"Don't wander off." Then he left her, alone in ancient Egypt in a temple desecrated by her enemy.

After hours of waiting, her patience vanished. The silence was making her nervous. She wondered if Carter had lost his courage and abandoned her after all.

As she started to stand up, something shifted inside her. Her body sensed danger. Her skin prickled, and cold terror swept up her spine. She pulled herself up, ready to run.

Hooves clopped down the corridor. There was no mistaking that sound.

Her heart raced. Maybe Carter hadn't lost his courage; maybe he had always intended to betray her.

She remembered how Shaitan had smelled her fear and sensed the beating of her heart. How could she hide from such powers? The only way she knew was to transform herself into a cobra, but she didn't have time, and what would happen if he caught her in the middle of her change?

The hoofbeats stopped. Seconds ticked by.

Dalila held her breath and waited, the tension within her growing. Finally, unable to bear the stress any longer, she crept around a column and looked down the corridor.

Shaitan stood unnaturally still. She knew intuitively that he sensed her nearby. His eyes shifted, and then his head turned toward her. He remained motionless, watching her, his nostrils wide, savoring the scent of her terror. She gazed at him transfixed, her mind beyond fear, her body numb.

He dropped to his hands, and for a moment, she thought he meant to crawl to her. Then his body, still in its human guise, became sleek, poised to attack, his arm muscles throbbing with power.

Someone grabbed her nightgown, yanking her back. Carter placed his hand over her mouth to silence her scream. She swallowed the cry and stared into his eyes.

"What are you doing?" he whispered harshly.

Shaitan snarled, and the corridor became filled with the horrible echo of running hooves.

Dalila didn't have the nerve or energy to run. Carter swept her into his arms and sprinted silently around the giant columns. He carried her out into the darkness.

When they were safely behind the gates of another temple, he set her down.

"I love you," he said, before he began intoning a spell.

Immediately, Dalila realized he was sending her back to the future. "I can't leave," she protested. "I have to steal the magic back before Shaitan uses it to summon Seth."

"If you stay here, your soul dies," Carter warned after he had finished the spell.

Blinding sunlight burst into the night. A bridge formed in front of Dalila, but this time she didn't run onto it.

Carter sensed her hesitation. "It's the only way to protect you, Dalila."

When she still didn't move, he lifted her into his arms again and carried her on to the bridge.

"Something's wrong." She struggled to free

herself from his hold. "Shaitan let us escape too easily."

"I conjured a dozen scents to confuse him," Carter explained. "He's probably still back in the temple, following the wrong one."

"But—"

"Can't you trust me after what I've done?" he asked. "I stole this incantation so you could escape."

Suddenly, she became more concerned for his safety than her own. "What will they do to you when they find out?"

"Maybe they never will," he replied.

The bridge began to slope downward. He set her on it.

"Please don't," she whimpered. "You don't understand. You're sending me back to Shaitan."

"You'll return to a later time," Carter said. "I promise. I made the necessary calculations and worked them into the spell." Then he ran back the way they had come and vanished in the darkness.

Suddenly, the path in front of Dalila tilted sharply, bending at a steep angle. She lost her footing and fell forward, sliding downward on her stomach, the wind racing through her hair. Adrenaline shot through her as the future raced up to meet her.

CHAPTER 14

Dalila landed with a jolt, collapsing on her bedroom floor. Her sudden arrival stirred the air. The skirt of her bedspread ballooned out before settling again. Exhausted, she rested her cheek against the carpet and listened. The house seemed eerily quiet. From the slant of sunlight falling across her face, she knew the day had passed.

Slowly, she sat up and groaned. Her muscles ached. A bruise was swelling on her left arm. And even though her energy was depleted, she knew she had to return to the past and stop Shaitan. If she failed—

"Stop!" she yelled, refusing to even consider what the world would become if she were unsuccessful.

Wearily, she rose to her feet. The papyrus that her uncle had given her still lay on the floor where she had dropped it that morning. A white envelope sat on her desk. She tore it open, slumped onto her bed, and read the letter that was inside.

Dear Dalila,

It has been my pleasure to be your companion and teacher over these past three years. I have come to love you, and so it is with great sadness that I will be giving your uncle my resignation.

For the longest time I have noticed curious things happening within your home. I ignored the way the fire in the hearth seemed to ignite on its own and the unnatural way a patch of sky cleared each night when your uncle retired to his study to gaze at the stars through his telescopes. I could list a dozen more occurrences. I kept telling myself that it was only my imagination, that I was being foolish, but after this morning, I realize that something more is happening here.

Let me assure you that your secret is safe with me. I assume that you are fighting some indefinably evil force and although I don't understand why you have been chosen for such a dreadful task, I do believe that the Divine Intelligence made the perfect choice in selecting you. I have come to know you as a clever and brave young woman, and I have every confidence that you will always do what is right.

Your uncle hired me to be your bodyguard as well as your tutor and chaperone. I'm not sure that you are aware of this. But it is true. I had assumed he was concerned that someone might try to kidnap you, but after this morning's encounter, I know that my skills and weaponry are not enough to protect you. The only thing I can do is light a candle each night and pray for you. That I will faithfully do.

Fondly,
Anita Lavendish

Just as Dalila finished reading the letter, the

telephone rang. The sudden noise startled her. She stared at the phone, remembering Shaitan speaking to her through the answering machine.

With a burst of fury, she lunged across the bed and picked up the receiver. She would not cower again. "Hello."

She had expected to hear Shaitan on the other end. Instead, her uncle's voice came across the line. "Dalila, thank God I caught you in time. Don't use the incantation I gave you. Promise me."

She paused, considering how much she should tell him. "Why not?"

"The incantation will take you back into the past," he explained.

"But you must have known that when you first gave it to me," she said. "What happened to change your mind?"

"The artifacts that the archaeologist found in the tomb, Levi buttons, and—" His voice faltered, and she wondered if he was crying. Maybe the pause was only caused by a glitch in the satellite connection. "—And the bracelet that Carter gave you—both of them were found on the floor in the burial chamber."

She froze, unable to breathe.

He went on, "I can't know that it's the same one, of course."

"It must be someone's idea of a joke," she answered stiffly, staring down at the gold chain encircling her wrist.

"That's what I told my colleagues, but the coincidence . . . I'm terrified. Promise me that you won't use the incantation."

"Don't worry," she said.

"That's not a promise," he scolded. "If you use the spell, I'm afraid you'll escape into the past only to meet your death there."

She closed her eyes.

"Swear to me," he said.

"I swear I won't use the incantation," she lied. "I'll put it away."

"I love you, Dalila," he whispered.

She set the phone back in its charger. She had no choice. She had to return and steal the magic, no matter what the cost. But death wasn't the worst thing that she would face. She shuddered, remembering what Carter had said: *if you stay here, your soul dies.*

$\mathbf{A}$s soon as Abdel opened his front door, Dalila rushed inside. "I need to talk to you." She felt dizzy from not eating or sleeping. When she latched on to his arm to steady herself, he stiffened. She glanced up. "What's wrong?"

He didn't seem happy to see her, maybe because he was dressed in shabby pajamas and looked drained. And then she remembered. "You said you wouldn't know me the next time you saw me."

He nodded. "I had assumed I wouldn't see you until"—he interrupted himself—"until later."

"I traveled back in time to ancient Egypt," she exclaimed, expecting shock to register on his face.

He remained motionless; the way he was staring at her was unnerving.

"Do you think I'm lying to you?" she asked.

He shook his head.

"Then?" She drew the word out, anticipating some comment from him.

The silence between them grew tense. She wanted to scream at him and force him to react. Instead, she closed the door with a slam that rattled the house.

"I'll start again." She went into the living room, surprised to find the room so cold. Smoke drifted about, floating in heavy layers. The fire had gone out, but some embers were still glowing. Without thinking, she started to speak the incantation her uncle used to rekindle a fire, but stopped when she sensed other magic in the air, its presence so strong she could almost taste its sweetness.

She glanced at Abdel. "Maybe you should rekindle the fire."

He didn't move.

"I'll do it, then." She grabbed the poker from the fire irons and angrily jabbed at a log. Sparks crackled and flew up the chimney. She added a few sticks, and soon a small fire burned fitfully.

Abdel still hadn't moved.

In the flickering light, Dalila could clearly see the living room now. Blankets were tangled on a chair, and a plate of scrambled eggs sat uneaten on a low table next to a full cup of coffee and a flat, shallow bowl filled with water.

"Do you have the flu?" she asked with concern. Her natural instinct was to take care of him. "Maybe you should sit down."

He moved woodenly across the floor and fell into the chair opposite her.

"We don't have much time," he said impatiently and gazed down at the bowl of water.

She wondered briefly what he had to do that was so urgent. "I don't care if I interfere with your plans," she said. "What you have to do can't possibly be more important that what I need to talk to you about."

"*You* don't have much time," he said, correcting her.

His words sent a chill through her. She stared back at him, then slowly, tremulously, began her story, avoiding any mention of Carter, not sure why she was protecting him. Maybe in a girlish way she hoped her love would be strong enough to make him quit the cult, even though reason told her that love alone could never make a person change.

When she had finished, her mouth felt dry. She reached across the table, picked up the cup, and sipped the cold coffee. The bitterness settled on her tongue, but the liquid soothed her. She set the cup down and glanced around. Incense was burning in a corner of the room. She had been so focused on telling her own story that she hadn't noticed it before.

At once she understood: Abdel hadn't forgotten to eat because he was ill; he had been using the surface of the water in the bowl to see into the future, and whatever he had seen had made him forget everything else. He had been compelled to light incense and pray.

"Do I fail to get the magic back?" she asked.

"Is that the reason you look so grim?"

He didn't answer.

"How much time do I have?" She waited nervously for his reply.

"None," he whispered, choking on the word. "It should have been done already."

She wondered if Carter had known this. Had he sent her back to the future not to protect her but to make sure she didn't stop the cult from freeing Seth?

"What should I have done?" she asked.

Abdel didn't answer. His fingers dug into the arms of the chair.

She joined him, standing behind his chair, and stared at the water. She couldn't see anything, but she assumed from Abdel's bleak expression that he saw a dismal, harsh future reflected on the surface.

"I don't think I'll survive the journey back unless you tell me what to do," she said softly. "Obviously, you know something."

He closed his eyes. "I know nothing that can help."

"I don't know how to control the magic," she confessed. "I'm afraid to touch it."

"The Enchantress should never be afraid," he instructed. "She has power over magic, even the remnants left from the earliest ages."

"But I don't know that I am the Enchantress," she muttered. "I don't feel strong." She pulled out the papyrus her uncle had given her. "I need to return to the exact time that I left. How can I be sure the incantation will take me back to the same place?"

"You must envision where you want to go," he answered.

"Envision Shaitan?" she asked hopelessly. "Can't you tell me another way?"

"Dalila, don't you . . . can't you . . ." He grimaced. "I gave you the only answer I can."

"Why won't you help me?" she asked.

"It's complicated," he said hoarsely. "More complicated than I can tell you right now."

"I'm supposed to die there, aren't I?" she said. "That's why you won't say anything, because you're afraid that if I learn the truth, then I won't have the courage to go back and do what is necessary."

He opened his mouth, then closed it without uttering a word.

"You needn't worry." She smiled thinly. "I'll sacrifice myself to save the world."

She stared into the fire. "I never really got to live the life I was given," she whispered. "This was the first time I've had friends my own age, and their friendship has given me so much joy. I hadn't known how much fun I was missing, and now, to lose it all . . ."

"Maybe you should take them with you," Abdel said.

"There's no reason for them to die, too," she argued. "I plan to go alone."

"You said they were your friends. They'll want to go with you," he countered.

"I can't ask them to go with me," she said firmly.

His posture changed. She saw a flicker of worry. He clenched his jaw, and then his face went blank again.

"Why should I take them with me?" she asked.

He let out a shuddering breath, but no words followed.

She was staggered by his silence, but at the same time she pitied him for the fear she saw in his eyes. Without saying good-bye, she left his house, dispirited by his refusal to help her.

When she stood on the sidewalk outside, she glanced back. Abdel was looking through the window, watching her. She stared at him, puzzling over what he had said. She didn't understand why he wanted her to take Sudi and Meri with her. She felt certain they wouldn't survive. Were three deaths needed to save the world?

Glittering angels circled overhead, gliding in and out of the long strips of silver cloth that hung from the skylight in the Building Museum. Dalila breathed in the scents of cologne and perfume and wished she could join the party. Instead, she stood like an orphan, dressed in her jeans and a sweater, watching the others dance. The music pulsed through her, a locomotive beat, heavy on the guitar, and her hips began to sway as she scanned the dancers, searching for Meri and Sudi.

Almost everyone wore a costume. A few had on white satin gowns and hid their faces behind saintly masks, while others looked like whimsical fairies with ornate jeweled wings that changed color in the flashing pink, purple, and blue lights. All of Sara's hard work had paid off; she had created an illusion of heaven, although a bizarrely rocker kind.

Dalila took a step toward the edge of the dance floor and caught a dark shadow from out of the corner of her eye.

Three guys dressed in black jeans, tux jackets, and concert T-shirts leaned against the stage, their hands in their pockets, trying hard to look bored. She recognized the tallest. Zack caught her staring at him and signaled to his friends to remain behind as he walked toward her with slow, lazy steps.

This time, she refused to be frightened away. She remained, rooted to the spot, defiantly returning his gaze.

"Party crashers," someone said, startling her.

Sara stood beside her. "Can you imagine? They just showed up, even though I didn't invite them." Red wings poked through her silky black cape. "How did they get past the security guard?"

"Maybe they hypnotized him," Dalila said vaguely.

Sara laughed good-naturedly. Tendrils of hair fell over her glossy cheek. "I know you let them in with you."

"Me?"

"It's all right." Sara placed a soft hand on Dalila's arm. "I don't care. Besides, they're Carter's friends. I figured they'd show up with or without an invitation."

"They're Carter's friends?" Dalila asked, even though she knew Sara had no reason to lie.

Sara gave her an odd look. "Didn't you know?"

"Is Carter here?" Dalila answered with a question of her own.

Sara tilted her head, and her skull earrings dangled against her thin throat. "Sorry," she said. "He's not coming."

Dalila finally noticed the costume Sara was wearing: a clinging black gown with a belt of rattling skulls. "What kind of angel are you?"

"I'm the angel of death, of course." Sara laughed again and strutted away, clearly enjoying her night. She stopped to talk to Dominique. Brian started dancing with them both. He wore a lopsided halo and cardboard wings that were spray-painted silver.

When Dalila turned around, she collided with Zack. She could feel the muscles in his chest. A chill raced through her, but not the pleasant kind.

"I'm Zack," he said with easy confidence. "Maybe Sudi told you."

Dalila jerked back. "You're not in costume, Zack," she said, feeling foolish for not being able to think of something more daring to say.

"I'm a fallen angel." He smirked and slid his hands down Dalila's arms. His touch was too familiar. She pulled away, but that only seemed to encourage him.

"Carter's not returning." He brazenly took her hand and placed it on his shoulder. Then he swayed, trying to force her to dance with him. His fingers found her waist and began sneaking under her sweater to her bare skin.

"He'll be back," Dalila countered. She was

determined not to let Zack get the better of her and untangled herself from his embrace with slow, strong movements.

"How can you be so sure?" he asked with a derisive smile, seeming to delight in the way he was flustering her.

"Because I'm the Enchantress," she answered boldly.

His expression changed. Had the word frightened him? Why would it? She pressed her palms against his chest and pushed him out of her way. This time he let her go. She circled the dance floor, continuing her search for Meri and Sudi.

"Dalila!" Sudi ran around the water fountain, waving her hand. Large feathered wings fluttered gracefully behind her.

"How did you get your wings to stay out?" Dalila asked.

"I've been practicing all week." Sudi looked upset and absently plucked a feather from her wing. "But I can't get them to go back in now. Do you think they're stuck this way?"

"If they are, you won't have to worry about college," Meri said, joining them, "because you can have a career, as a bird-girl with Ripley's Believe It or Not."

"That's not funny." Sudi rolled her eyes, then quickly changed the subject. "Dalila, where have you been? We've been looking for you all day."

"I've been . . ." Dalila paused, unsure of what to say.

"We wanted you to get ready with us." Meri twirled to show off her silky halter dress. Pale green wings with long, delicate tails like those of a luna moth were glued on to her bare back. "My stylist brought over the greatest dresses."

"Isn't she gorgeous?" Sudi said. "And I love the curls." She playfully tousled Meri's black hair.

Dalila felt suddenly selfish. She couldn't take her friends back to the past with her. She never should have come looking for them.

"You both look great," she said, trying to think up an excuse so she could leave. "Let me go home and change—" She turned abruptly, searching for the exit.

Meri slipped in front of her and blocked her way. "We know that look. What happened?"

"Nothing." Dalila tried to dodge around her, but Sudi stopped her this time.

"You're not good at lying at all. Tell us," Sudi demanded. Her eyes darted toward the stage where Zack stood with his friends. "It's something bad, or *they* wouldn't be here. What made them decide to show up like they own the world?"

"Maybe because they think they will," Dalila said sorrowfully.

Meri and Sudi pulled her away from the dance floor.

"Tell us everything," Sudi said.

"I needed Abdel's help," Dalila said, not sure where to begin. "So I went over to his house. He didn't tell me what to do, but he suggested in a roundabout way that—"

"I thought he said he wouldn't know us the next time we saw him," Meri interrupted.

"He knew me, and he wasn't happy to see me," Dalila said. "He thought I should take you with me, but I can see now that he was wrong."

"Take us where?" Meri and Sudi asked in unison.

"Ancient Egypt," Dalila answered. The words

were out, though she wished she could pull them back, because Sudi and Meri didn't look afraid; they looked thrilled.

"Into the past?" Meri said excitedly. "You mean, like time-traveling?"

"The magic from the papyrus I destroyed is there," Dalila explained. "At least, I think it is. Shaitan has it, and I need to go back and steal it from him before he can use it to summon Seth."

Dalila became silent, unable to say more, because Michelle had suddenly pushed her way into their circle. She was dressed like a devil. Sparkling horns peeked out from her golden curls.

"Why are the three of you always hunched together telling secrets?" She folded her arms over her sequined gown, expecting an answer. When no one spoke, she went on. "You know, everyone is talking about the strange way the three of you are always off by yourselves, whispering together."

"Get real, Michelle," Sudi said. "No one's worried about it except for you. Are you so paranoid that you think we're talking about you?"

"The envy of others is a problem I've had to deal with all my life," Michelle said haughtily.

Sudi opened her mouth to reply, but Michelle unexpectedly focused her attention on Dalila.

"Why aren't you wearing a costume?" Michelle asked. "I mean, usually your style is passable, but you didn't even try tonight; you're still in your jeans."

"You should talk, Michelle," Sudi said. "Wasn't the idea to dress like an angel?"

"Please," Michelle sniffed. "What do you think the devil is? Just an angel who refused to bow." A sly smile formed on her lips. "I bet even the devil would bow to me tonight. I look beautifully wicked, and I know it."

She tilted her head and caught sight of Zack. She stood up straighter and smoothed her hands down her sides. "I love bad boys. I'm going to introduce myself. Want to come and watch my flirting style?"

Dalila pulled her back.

"Cecil has been staring at you all night," Sudi said, helping Dalila steer Michelle in the opposite direction. "Go on a mission of mercy, and ask him to dance." Cecil was the son of the Romanian ambassador. Lots of girls had crushes on him, but he remained infatuated with Michelle.

"He is incredible, isn't he?" Michelle sighed. "You're right." She left them and sauntered over to Cecil.

"Can you even imagine if Michelle joined the cult?" Meri said. "Abdel was right. We need to go back and stop Shaitan before he uses the magic to summon Seth. I can feel something bad in the air; power is shifting already."

Dalila sensed something brewing. She looked around the room but doubted others noticed it. They were too busy partying.

"Can we at least wait until the party is over?" Sudi asked, staring longingly at Scott. He wore a tux and a silky black shirt underneath. He looked classy, even with the tiny fairy wings tied around his shoulders.

"There won't be a party if Seth comes back," Meri answered. "The future will change. We might not even exist."

"But what if we get stuck there?" Sudi asked. "You two can fit in, but what about me?" She held out a strand of her white-blond hair.

"We won't stay there," Meri replied. "Not if

Dalila is along. Remember when Anubis sent us to hell?"

"Dalila got us out." Sudi brightened. "Okay. Let's get it over with. Maybe we can get back in time for a good-night kiss, at least." She glanced back at Scott and sighed. "I think we better sneak out. I have a creepy feeling that Zack and his friends are here to stop us from leaving."

They headed toward the side entrance, where the catering company had set up a tent. Then they stole through the kitchen to the outside, where they huddled together for warmth. Dalila took the papyrus her uncle had given her from her pocket and began reciting the praises to Amun-Re.

"Sudi!" someone yelled at the same moment that Dalila completed the spell.

Sunlight flared and ripped a hole in the night. Dazzling light blinded them and warmed the air. The sunbeams pulled together, melding into golden stones. Within seconds a bridge lay in front of them.

Dalila started over it.

Sudi caught Dalila's arm and pulled her back. "It's Scott."

"We'll worry about explaining this to him

when we get back," Dalila said. "Right now we need to hurry. The bridge disappears quickly."

"He's coming with us," Meri said.

Dalila whipped around.

Scott stood next to Sudi, his fists on his hips. "Wow," he said, looking dumbfounded. "Sara is incredible. How did she do this? It looks like a gateway to heaven."

CHAPTER 17

"The bridge is the biggest surprise of the party," Dalila lied to Scott. "You're not supposed to know about it yet."

"Why not?" He tried to step around Dalila, but she bumped against him, blocking his way. Then she smiled sweetly, and both she and Meri shoved him back.

He was taken by surprise and lost his balance. His hands swung out as he tried to stop his fall, but he tumbled backward anyway, hitting the grass with a soft thump.

"Maybe I was wrong," Sudi said, placing her arm around Dalila. "You're getting pretty good at lying."

"I don't know if that's something to be proud of," Dalila said, but then she smiled, because, strangely, she was.

Meri pointed down. "We'd better hurry."

The bridge was disappearing. Scott had made the girls linger too long.

"Go!" Dalila cried as she dashed forward. She pumped her arms at her sides, trying to outrun the darkness that was advancing behind her. Meri and Sudi sprinted ahead of her, their long dresses swishing about their legs, their heels tapping out a rapid staccato beat.

Dalila raced after them. She went through everything in her mind and, with a jolt, realized she didn't know if they were heading toward the right time and place; they could end up in a swamp surrounded by dinosaurs. Abdel had told her to envision where she wanted to go. She needed to find Shaitan so she could steal back the magic, but thinking about him only renewed her fear.

She tried to visualize the mist, then concentrated on the temple with the massive pillars that she had been in with Carter. But fear and exhaustion were finally taking their toll. Her tired mind worked clumsily; she couldn't focus. Pictures of Shaitan, Carter, and even the crocodile attack flicked through her thoughts.

Against her will, her steps slowed. She couldn't go on. Her side ached. Her head was spinning. She closed her eyes, trying to overcome the pain; then, resting her hands on her knees, she leaned over. Her skin prickled with sweat. She felt hot and knew she was going to pass out.

"Freaky," Meri said.

Dalila opened her eyes. The bridge had disappeared. She stood on parched desert land. A scorpion scuttled across the sand in front of her.

She dropped her hands and stood up very slowly, willing the dizziness to go away. They were near the Nile, on the west bank. The temples and tombs of the necropolis lay ahead of them. Boats glided across the water, and in the distance, farther down the river, she saw the papyrus swamp and knew they had returned to the funerary complex she had visited before.

"This is the right place," she said with relief.

"Good." Sudi marched toward the massive pylons and statues. "Now all we have to do is find the magic and steal it back."

"Just think of the power we have," Meri said excitedly, skipping along beside Sudi. "One sneeze and we could change history. If I had a cold, I could create an epidemic and wipe out the world population. Even the smallest thing . . . like, if we just left a simple equation on one of the temple walls, or—"

"Maybe I misjudged Abdel," Dalila interrupted softly. "Suppose he couldn't help us because he knew if he did, he might accidentally change the future."

"That's no excuse," Sudi said angrily. "He should have told us what to do."

"This trip back in time is just happening for us," Dalila explained, surprised to find herself defending Abdel. "But in reality, our visit here has already shaped history. We've done what we're supposed to do, and if we don't repeat it precisely now, then the outcome could change. Maybe Abdel was afraid that if he gave us any advice, we might do something that could have a terrible effect on the future."

"So anything we do here could change things?" Sudi asked, and, without waiting for an answer, she grinned mischievously. "Let's write our alphabet across a wall, so that years from now archaeologists can puzzle over it and wonder why the ancient Egyptians used their hieroglyphs, and not the ABC's."

Dalila hung back as Meri and Sudi trudged ahead, their dresses flapping in the breeze. She could hear their laughter as they continued to scheme.

Across the river, a funeral cortege moved to the water's edge. Women, probably professional mourners, wailed and shouted lamentations, while beating their breasts. Others fell to their knees and struck their heads repeatedly on the ground. Servants carried food and furniture destined to be buried with the deceased for use in the afterlife.

Dalila watched until an odd breeze caught her attention.

Behind her the wind had stirred the sand,

swirling it into a reddish brown cloud. A vague figure pulled itself together within it, man-size, but not a man: a grotesque shape, half monster, half goat, walked through the storm.

Then the wind died down, the sand settled, and Shaitan strode toward Dalila.

Frantically, she intoned the protective spell. The scorching wind tore the words from her lips. An orange glow formed into a raggedly trembling mass. She swung her arm out and sent the magic to shield Meri and Sudi.

Shaitan raised his hand, and the orange cloud created from Dalila's spell burst into a thousand black fragments that became buzzing flies.

Meri and Sudi screamed and batted at the insects circling around them.

Dalila started to run, but Shaitan captured her and pulled her against his body. She twisted and pulled away from him, trying to break free, but his fingers only dug in tighter.

He snickered. "Enchantress," he said against her cheek. His hot breath steamed over her. "Your power is great, and soon you will use it to summon my god Seth, the lord of chaos."

Meri and Sudi rushed back to rescue her.

"Don't," Dalila whispered weakly. "Run."

Two priests wearing cloaks made from leopard skins suddenly appeared. Their heads were shaven, and thick black kohl lined their eyes. Both wore pectoral ornaments decorated with images of Seth, the god with the snout of an anteater and rectangular ears. They captured Meri and Sudi and then escorted all three girls toward the temple.

When they passed through the first pylon, more priests joined the procession led by Shaitan. The girls hooked arms and squeezed together.

Sudi giggled, her chest vibrating.

"Stop it," Dalila warned.

Sudi was becoming wildly emotional because of the stress. "I can't help it." She leaned into Dalila. "I have never seen a man as ugly as Shaitan. He must be what my grandmother means when she calls something 'as ugly as sin.'"

Dalila tried to shush her again. "Be quiet. He'll hear you."

"He looks like a goat," Meri added, and she laughed so hard she sprayed spittle on the back of the priest in front of them.

"Stop," Dalila cautioned, her fear rising to a new level of terror. "Don't taunt him."

"Just use your papyrus to take us back," Meri said. "I'm ready to go home."

Shaitan stopped abruptly. His head swiveled around.

Dalila groaned.

He walked back to her. "What papyrus would that be?" he asked.

Dalila shook her head. "I don't know what she's talking about," Dalila lied. "You heard her. Fear is making her giddy. She's hysterical."

Shaitan studied Dalila. Then his thick, callused hand shot out. His fingers dug into her jeans pocket and snatched the papyrus. He held it up, scanning the hieroglyphs. "This is what you don't know about, so you won't miss it." He pinched the papyrus between two of his fingers and blew on it. It smoldered before bursting into flames.

Hot ash floated into the air and fell on Dalila's face.

Meri embraced Dalila and began to cry.

Sudi collapsed on the ground. "How are we going to get home now?"

"Why did you bring your friends back with you, Dalila?" Shaitan grasped Sudi's throat, forcing her to stand. "They'll only be in the way, and now I'll have to dispose of them."

Dalila wrapped her arm around Sudi and continued to hold Meri against her. "We'll get out of this," she whispered, even though she knew no words could comfort them. "Don't worry."

"It's Abdel's fault," Meri said, her chest convulsing with sobs. "Why didn't he help us?"

The procession began again. Shaitan led them past the massive columns and into the inner sanctuary. The cauldron with the magic was there. The mist rippled, then rose, quivering with excitement, seeming to recognize Dalila.

"Use the magic, and free my lord of chaos," Shaitan ordered.

The priests eased back, and so did Shaitan. Dalila had an uneasy feeling that they had already tried to use the magic and failed. Their eyes settled on her, their expressions fervent, anticipating something momentous.

"I don't know how," Dalila said honestly.

"Of course you do." Sudi nudged her. "If

Shaitan is afraid of it, then it must be something you can use against him."

"How?" Dalila asked. "They may call me the Enchantress, but that doesn't mean I know what to do."

"Try anything." Meri pushed her forward. "What do we have to lose?"

Dalila stared down at the mist. It had retreated to the bottom of the vessel and tightened itself into a silver puddle that could have fit into the palm of her hand. This close, she could smell its odd metallic odor and feel the cold wafting off it. She sensed it was pure evil and wondered again why Shaitan wasn't able to use it to summon Seth.

Tentatively, she touched it. It bit her, nipping the tip of her finger. A drop of her blood fell on it. It keened hungrily, eager for more, and shot up again as a mist, facing her. She stared, transfixed. It grew until it was looming over her. She wondered how members of the cult had been able to capture it; it seemed too powerful for anyone to control.

Shaitan growled, warning Dalila to be cautious.

She raised her hand, then slowly lowered it,

testing. The mist shuddered, but obeyed her, following the direction of her finger. It bowed to her, then curled back inside its vessel, whimpering.

She lifted her hand again, and the mist seemed to grow impatient. A tendril stretched out and touched the tip of her finger, licking her skin and leaving it wet and numb with cold. The mist tried to wrap itself around her hand, but from deep within it, Dalila heard the faint screams of others who had tried to tame it and failed. The cries were distant, but she knew that they were the thin, tortured sounds of others who had let the mist claim them.

With tremendous effort, she drew back; part of her wanted to join the mist, to crawl inside it and be swept away. She knew that if she had let it embrace her, it would have stolen her life, and a strange death would have come quickly; Dalila would have been imprisoned within it, conscious but no longer able to control, or even influence, her existence. That gave her an idea. Could she do it?

Without thinking, she brought her hand down. When the mist coiled back into a ball of silver, she scooped it out of the vessel, cupped it in her palm, and hurled it at Shaitan.

CHAPTER 18

The priests were ready for Dalila's betrayal. They threw a net and caught the mist before it touched Shaitan. Amulets and charms hung from every knot in the mesh, and when the objects touched the mist, they glowed and sparked; some even caught fire. Red flames hissed, and the air filled with the acrid smell of smoke.

Dalila could see now that the magic wasn't exactly a mist after all, but a formless entity, something sentient and alive, with a ferocious will to survive. It snarled and fought the net, but the criss-cross threads held.

The more the mist bucked and strained, the more the netting tightened around it. At last, with a mournful cry that sounded almost human, it shrank back and lay still. The priest carried it to the vessel and carefully shook it loose from the net. It slipped inside the bowl and lay in the bottom, a silver liquid again, swishing unhappily back and forth.

Dalila sensed that it was gazing at her somehow, even though it had no eyes. Still, its attention was fixed on her, watching her. She dreamily stared back at it.

For one confused moment she thought she heard Meri and Sudi calling to her, warning her to look away, but they sounded so distant, their voices growing muffled until she could no longer hear them. Her attention returned lovingly to the mist. It might once have been one of the fiery spirits that had existed before creation, but the poor thing that languished before her now was nothing to be afraid of. What was so horrible about it that even the devil feared it?

She sensed the way it yearned for freedom. All it really wanted was to go home and be with its own kind, to love and be loved. Maybe, she should release it. After all, it was only a force; when harnessed, it could be used for good or bad. The magic itself was faultless.

It stirred and rose up to the ceiling, luminous and pleasing to look at. A thought drifted lazily across her mind: if she took a deep breath, she could inhale it and become one with it. She felt it bending toward her, eager for their union.

Shaitan squeezed her shoulder, pulling her back. For a few seconds, he said nothing. He merely restrained her.

Gradually, Dalila came to her senses. "It hypnotized me, didn't it?" she said.

"You felt its power," Shaitan whispered. "Either you will use it, or it will use you. You are the Enchantress. You have no other choice."

"I won't use the magic to summon Seth," she declared.

"Perhaps another Enchantress will be born who is willing," Shaitan said. "I can wait. I have eternity."

Two priests stepped forward and took Dalila's arms. They dragged her outside. Sudi and Meri followed close behind, guarded by four more priests.

The sun was balanced on the western horizon, making their shadows stretch across the rock-strewn desert as they marched down into a ravine and continued on until they reached a royal burial site. There they entered a tomb cut into a cliff.

The priests led them down a long corridor. When they passed a wall painting of the king lassoing a bull, Dalila realized they were walking in the very tomb that her uncle was excavating four thousand years in the future. She remembered her uncle's warning and frantically looked around for a way to escape.

She wondered what had happened to Carter. She expected him to dart out from a hiding place and rescue her, but when the priests took her into the burial chamber, she lost all hope. She stared at Meri and Sudi, feeling utter despair.

The mourners had left loaves of bread and jugs of beer around the sarcophagus. The yeasty scents crowded the room and overwhelmed the smoky incense that had been lit earlier.

"No wonder tomb robbers were willing to risk their souls to steal these treasures," Sudi said. "Look at the jewelry."

An array of gold and precious stones glinted around them. The craftsmanship in the cosmetics chest and ceremonial chair was breathtaking.

A priest began snuffing out the flames of the few wicks still burning in the oil lamps. When the room was dark, the priests filed back into the antechamber. The last one closed the doors behind him.

The girls stood in the darkness, linking arms, and listened to the wet scraping of mortar across the door as the mason sealed them inside the tomb.

CHAPTER 19

Silence wrapped around them, thick and heavy. The utter darkness gave Dalila the sense of being blind. She wished she had never asked Meri and Sudi to come back with her. She had only brought them to an unimaginably horrible death. How long would it take before the air inside the tomb became too poisoned to breathe?

"I'm not going to die standing up," Sudi announced. Her words echoed oddly about the room. A shuffling sound followed as Sudi sat down.

Dalila and Meri joined her on the floor. They kicked the loaves of bread out of their way and leaned against one another.

"How long do you think it will take, you know, before we . . . ?" Meri didn't finish her question.

Dalila couldn't bear to answer her. She shrugged, even though she knew Meri couldn't see her response.

Meri sniffled and rested her head on Dalila's lap.

Silence fell over them again.

After a few moments, Sudi broke the quiet. "I wish I'd been nicer to my twin sisters."

"Maybe you'll still have a chance," Dalila said, trying to sound optimistic, though her voice had lost its strength. Her shoulders slumped. "I never got to tell my uncle how grateful I am for—"

A scraping sound captured her attention. Her heart skipped a beat as she listened. There it was again: a faint scratching within the chamber walls. She imagined starving rats or jackals scrabbling at the limestone, determined to break in.

"What is it?" Meri sat up.

"Maybe animals are trying to get in," Dalila whispered, doing her best to contain her excitement.

Sudi scooted closer. "But if they make a tunnel to get in, then maybe we can use it to get out."

"Exactly," Dalila said.

Moments passed.

"I don't hear anything," Sudi said anxiously.

"It'll come," Meri said. "Maybe they had to push rubble out of the way."

"Can animals do that?" Sudi asked.

"Who cares?" Meri said irritably. "As long as we get out, does it matter?"

The sound began again. The girls froze, listening closely, taking their breaths in slow quiet draws. There was urgency about the scratching this time. Soon, the scraping took on a steady rhythm, but then, abruptly, it stopped.

Minutes went by. Dalila feared the animal had given up.

At last, the noise came again. This time, it was louder, almost grating, and seemed close by.

A loud crack startled Dalila. Something fell on the floor. The object bounced once, then settled near the girls.

"What was that?" Meri asked.

"The plaster," Sudi whispered anxiously. "What else can it be?"

All three girls stood up. They found one another's hands and pinched one another's fingers, silently communicating their readiness to fight any beast and claim the tunnel for themselves.

A fire poked through the wall, surprising them. They stumbled back.

Flames danced from the end of a torch. Smoke curled up, blackening the paintings above it. The holder of the torch tossed it into the room. The blaze landed on top of two loaves of bread and filled the room with the smell of burning toast.

"Someone's breaking in," Dalila whispered, her hope soaring. Maybe Carter was rescuing her after all.

"Tomb robbers," Meri whispered nervously. "Do you think they'll help us?"

"We'll make them," Sudi said. "They don't have a choice." And in the flickering firelight, her face looked determined.

More plaster crumbled, and then a head poked through the opening. Long hair hid the face. Hands appeared next and grasped the sides of the tunnel.

Dalila waited tensely.

The person slid down the side of the wall, braced his hands on the floor, and tumbled into the room.

He picked up the torch, unmindful of the girls' presence, and smiled with delight at the gold reflecting the firelight. He was barefoot and wore only a loincloth. A small pouch was strapped over his dark, muscular back.

He pushed the tangled hair out of his eyes, then lifted the torch higher and turned to survey the room. His dust-caked face was clearly visible now.

"Abdel!" Meri yelled. The first to recognize him under the dirt, she screamed with joy and ran toward him. Her arms flew open for a hug.

Abdel froze.

"You've come to save us!" Sudi shouted. In her excitement, her wings fluttered, stirring up a breeze.

Abdel dropped the torch and reeled, trying to flee, but instead he crashed into the huge sarcophagus. He turned back to face the girls and began shrieking loud, earsplitting cries for help.

Meri stopped. "What's wrong?"

He fumbled in his pouch, pulled out a clay jar, scooped his fingers inside, and threw a yellowish brown glob of something at her. It splattered across Meri's face.

"Yuck." Meri wiped her hands over her cheeks. "What is this?" She looked down at the thick, sticky liquid covering her fingers.

"He doesn't know us," Sudi squealed.

Abdel flung more of the gooey stuff at Sudi. The mess dripped over her lips. "It's sweet," she said, surprised.

"It's honey," Dalila said. The tension broke, and a flood of giggles erupted from her.

"Why is he throwing honey on us?" Meri asked, dismayed, cleaning her fingers with her tongue.

Abdel held more honey in his hand, ready to throw it.

"In ancient Egypt, honey was considered a poison for ghosts and evil spirits," Dalila explained. "And the two of you definitely look like winged creatures from the Netherworld."

Meri smirked. "He thinks we're demons, guarding the pharaoh's tomb."

"No wonder he's afraid." Sudi walked over to a wall. "Look at what's written here." She drew her finger over the hieroglyphs and in the dim firelight read aloud, "Anyone thinking of robbing this tomb, beware. The dead person is now capable of taking revenge and will kill the robber and ruin his whole family. A crocodile will be against him in the water, a snake on the land—"

Abdel cried out and sank to his knees. The clay jar broke, and honey oozed across the floor. His screaming kept Sudi from reading more.

"He thinks you're reading the curse to him," Dalila said, surprised that he could understand them; suddenly it occurred to her that they had been speaking in a different language since arriving in the past.

"I can't believe that this is the same Abdel we know," Meri said, bemused. "At least this explains why he was so upset when he read the incantation on your papyrus. He must have known that we were going to find out about his disreputable past as a tomb robber."

"Maybe we're the ones who made him change and live an honest life," Dalila said.

Abdel cowered, terrified, and remained that way for minutes. His stooped posture and intense shivering made Dalila feel sorry for him. She took his chin in her hand and forced him to gaze into her eyes. "Help us get out of the tomb," she said.

"I will be honored to help the magnificent demons." Abdel bowed until his forehead touched the floor. "But what kind of demons are you that you can't leave on your own power?"

"We're the kind who like to torture men who don't obey us." Sudi strutted back and forth, enjoying her demon role. "So, help us, or suffer."

"We can leave through the tunnel I dug," he said, his lips almost brushing the floor. He ventured a glance up.

"We need other clothes to wear," Meri said. "We can't go wandering around dressed like we are now and scare everyone."

Abdel tentatively lifted his head. "I can help."

He wiped his hands on his loincloth, then stood and scrambled over to a chest, opened it, and pulled out several long pieces of white linen. "These were meant for the pharaoh's queen to wear in the afterlife. They will look beautiful on demons."

He displayed one section of fabric across his arms and audaciously looked up at Meri. "Undress."

She gawked at him.

"Take off your clothes." He bowed. "I will dress you."

"Give me that." She tore the linen from his hands and unfolded it; then, puzzling over it, she glanced at Dalila. "Do you know how this works?"

Dalila shrugged.

"You are a demon," Abdel said with a cunning smile. "You can make me forget that I have seen your heavenly body."

Meri gave Dalila and Sudi a pleading look. "I'm not wearing a bra."

Dalila shrugged. "He seems determined. Besides, the ancient Egyptians didn't have the same fears about showing their bodies the way we do. Women worked topless, and sometimes even naked."

Sudi gave Meri an apologetic look. "We have to get out of here. I'm willing to do anything." She began stripping off her dress. "Besides, I don't see that we have much choice."

"All right, then." Meri tore off the wings glued

to her back as Sudi concentrated and pulled her own wings back into her body.

Abdel screamed again, but he forgot his fear once Meri's dress fell to the floor. She stood in front of him, waiting. After a pause, he began delicately wrapping her in the linen.

Dalila slipped out of her Levis and glanced down at them crumpled on the floor, knowing that in the future, archaeologists excavating this site would find them and call her uncle in a panic. Then, with a gasp, she saw the bracelet Carter had given her. The clasp had broken, and the chain had fallen from her wrist. She knew she had to leave it. Her hands had to be free for her to make her way through the tunnel. Maybe her uncle would bring it back to her.

She pulled on the pleated linen gown and felt herself blush. The fabric was see-through, and even though she had left on her underwear, she felt uncomfortable. She slipped into royal sandals that had images of the enemies of the kingdom painted on the innersoles.

Sudi studied the small opening in the wall. "Who wants to go first?"

"Wait!" Abdel smiled broadly and, unembarrassed, stripped off the coarse cloth that was wrapped around his hips.

"Wow." Sudi stared. "He's got a nice butt."

Meri smiled wickedly. "I can't wait to tell him what you just said when we see him again in the future."

Abdel pulled on the long white *shend'ot* meant for the pharaoh. He beamed and rubbed his hands over the fine material. "Now I look worthy enough to be in the company of demons."

Abdel stepped over to the break in the wall and pulled the linen up around his waist. He lifted himself into the tunnel and squirmed into the darkness.

Dalila wriggled in after him. Dirt and pebbles fell on her face. She closed her eyes and tried to block the memory of her parents' deaths in a tunnel like this one that had collapsed on top of them. Dust choked her. She could barely breathe. She crawled forward and then, without warning, banged her head against the rocks. Pain shot through her. She put her hand out to find her way again. The tunnel narrowed. She bent lower, then stretched her body until she was worming through the utter darkness. How had Abdel had been able to do this? He was much larger, his shoulders broad. She tried to squeeze her way forward; then, twisting, she turned onto her side, but it was no use. She was stuck.

Sudi tapped the bottom of Dalila's sandal. "Dalila, would you move it? I want to get out of here."

Dalila braced her feet against either side of the tunnel and pushed. She slid an inch, maybe two, scraping her cheek and shoulder on a jagged outcropping. Then she stopped, her body sandwiched between the rocks. She clawed at the sides of the tunnel, trying to find something to grasp on to.

"I can't!" she yelled back to Sudi.

Suddenly, Abdel's strong hands grasped her wrists and dragged her out into the moonlit night. She landed on her knees, crying out half in pain, half in joy, and then drew in huge gulps of air.

She jumped up to help Abdel pull Sudi from the hole. Sudi was covered with dust, and a cut on her arm was bleeding. Dalila hugged her. Then they turned to help Meri.

Rumbling from deep inside the tunnel shook the ground.

"Meri?" Dalila called tentatively as the earth continued vibrating beneath her feet.

Dust puffed from the mouth of the hole. Then rocks crashed down and shot out at them.

Abdel pushed Dalila aside and dived into the opening, but a flood of debris shoved him back out.

The tunnel had collapsed on Meri.

Recklessly, Dalila gripped stone after stone and threw them behind her, trying to dig Meri out. She snatched at rocks until her fingers were bleeding, but each time she removed one, a dozen more slid down to replace it.

Abdel and Sudi worked beside her, frantically digging in the rubble. Fragments of limestone covered their feet. More sharp-edged pieces of masonry clattered down on top of them.

"We have to save her," Dalila rasped, but her chest was already filling with heartsick despair. She felt suddenly too dizzy to stand. This couldn't be happening.

They had lost Meri.

CHAPTER 20

As dust continued to settle, Dalila remembered another cave-in: the one that had killed her parents when she was seven years old. Workmen had screamed their grief and tugged at the rocks in their futile attempts to rescue her parents.

"Rekhet. Rekhet." The word had resounded around her while she watched, a child then, helpless to do anything more than cry. The men digging into the wreckage had called her mother Rekhet. The name implied that she had powers beyond this

world. *Rekhet* meant "the knowing one"—a wise woman, a female who could talk with the dead, with spirits, with—

Dalila tore herself away from her thoughts. Her heart hammered painfully, and sweat prickled her forehead. She stirred the sand in front of her, willing herself not to remember, not to think.

But another image came, uninvited, this one of the small golden box from which her uncle had taken the papyrus. The image forced itself into the front of her mind. The words *Hery Seshta* had been written on the lid. The hieroglyphs stood for "the one who understands the mysteries." Her uncle had said that the box and incantation had been in their family since ancient times, so she must have been descended from people who possessed supernatural powers.

Maybe her ancestors were the ones who had tamed the fiery spirits that had existed before creation. Shaitan believed she had that kind of gift. He called her the Enchantress.

Another childhood memory pushed into her thoughts: she had spent hours learning spells, the way other children learned nursery rhymes.

She jumped up and started pacing, cursing her uncle for allowing her to believe that she was to marry a prince, and not forcing her to accept the truth.

"Dalila?" Sudi tried to put her arm around Dalila and comfort her.

But Dalila violently pushed her away. Her anger needed release. "What good is magic if I can't use it to save a friend?" Dalila asked, furious not with Sudi but with herself. "They call me the Enchantress, and I can't even help Meri."

Sudi held out her hands, palms up. "Abdel didn't teach us," she said mournfully. "We don't have—"

"That's your excuse." Dalila whipped around, unable to look at Sudi's sad face. "It's not mine. I could . . . I have . . ."

She raked her hand through her hair. She'd always been afraid to use her power, terrified of what existed inside her. She had considered it her dark side, and had pushed it out of consciousness, because it had frightened her. And worse, her uncle had let her; that was his sin. He never should have allowed her to consider the other side of her personality evil. In doing so, she had disowned her true identity. She had suppressed what she really was: the Enchantress. She had imprisoned herself in the foolish idea that her power would come to her only after she married a prince.

Outraged, she raised her hands to the star-filled sky and screamed the secret name of Atum-Re.

The night sky quaked. The stars quivered.

Abdel fell to the ground and dug his fingers into the dirt as if he thought the world were tilting and he needed to hold on so he wouldn't slide off. He looked up, terrified, and watched her.

Dalila spun around and faced the piles of stones. She spoke the words she had been too terrified to speak years ago over another mass of rocks, that had taken the lives of her parents.

"I-a un-a em sa-k hun-na-k nifu er fet k!" she shouted. "I have come that I may be your protector; I send wind for you to breathe."

As she finished the incantation, wind shrieked down from the East. The rocks rattled and crashed against one another.

Dalila waited, biting her lip. She had given

Meri air to breathe. Now she prayed that Meri still had the will to live.

An unmistakable meow filled the night.

Sudi cried out. She and Dalila ran back to the mound of rocks and began digging at what would have been Meri's grave.

Abdel joined them. He bent over, scooping armloads of stones out of the way.

A tiny cat poked through the wreckage, then burrowed out. The cat looked up at them and mewed plaintively.

Dalila picked up the dirty animal and cuddled it against her cheek, kissing the side of its body. Then Sudi took it and petted it, cooing sweet words into its ear.

Abdel watched, mystified.

"I think she's ready," Dalila said.

Sudi set the small cat down and stepped back. Immediately, its tail rippled and began to shrink. It bent over in pain, then yowled and stretched, forming sensuous arms and a tight stomach, the hips of a girl, and long black hair.

After a moment, Meri stood before them naked, her skin scratched and bruised; but she was wondrously alive. She squinched her eyes in concentration. The linen that Abdel had wrapped around her reappeared.

Sudi and Dalila embraced her.

"I'm so glad you're back." Sudi choked on a sob.

Dalila kissed Meri's cheek.

"I thought I'd died," Meri murmured.

"Maybe you just visited the other side," Dalila said. She could feel her confidence eroding. She prayed she had done the right thing.

"If it was your time to die," Sudi said firmly, looking at Dalila, "no amount of magic could have brought you back."

"Magic?" Meri whispered. "I thought the rocks shifted."

"They did." Dalila let out a long sigh. Already she could feel herself returning to the person she had been. Only the fear of Meri's death had forced her to reach so deep inside herself.

"Still, I think I went to another place." Meri had a strange, pensive look.

"Your brain was probably starved for oxygen," Dalila offered.

But Meri remained visibly shaken. "A woman who called herself Rekhet—"

Dalila took a sharp breath.

"I saw her in this other place," Meri went on. "She had a message for you, Dalila. She said the magic you're facing is unforgiving and has a long memory. It knows who you are. It's been an enemy of your family since the beginning. She wants you to take pen and ink—"

Sudi hugged Meri so tightly she couldn't say another word. "See, it was only a weird dream. You didn't die. Something must have knocked you in the head, and you were unconscious. Why would anyone suggest you use pen and ink to fight magic? Does that make any sense?"

Meri shrugged and smiled. "But it felt so real."

"We need to find the temple of Anubis." Dalila turned to Abdel. "Can you help us?"

Even in the milky glow of moonlight, she could see him blanch.

"Bad things happen there," he said. "It's a place that's dangerous for everyone, even demons. The priests—"

"We know," Sudi cut in. "You've already told us."

"When did I tell you?" Abdel looked worried. "It's not safe to speak the name of Anubis anymore."

"Just take us to the temple," Meri pleaded.

"You demons sometimes talk like you know me," Abdel ventured.

"In the future we do," Dalila said.

"Four thousand years from now," Sudi put in.

"Four thousand?" Abdel appeared even more unsettled. "No one lives that long except in the afterlife."

"We need to find the temple," Dalila reminded him, feeling cross from hunger and lack of sleep.

Abdel nodded, then looked at each one of them, studying the dirt caked on their skin and clothes. "We'll need to bathe first."

Impatiently, Dalila cast a spell to clean their clothes and bodies. In an instant, the air stirred. Wind caressed them with soft sweeping strokes and wiped away the dust and grime.

"I could get used to this." Sudi leaned back, clearly enjoying herself. Her hair flowed around her head as a breeze combed through it, untangling snarls and leaving it smooth and glossy.

Clean again, Meri seemed to regain her vivacity. "I think I did see the other world," she began as they followed Abdel across the pale, moonlit desert.

By the time they had reached the edge of the flood plain, Meri had finished her story. Her experience, whether it was real or not, gave Dalila comfort; she wanted to believe that the loving spirits of her parents were guiding her.

Unexpectedly, Abdel became more cautious. He crouched down low and scuttled behind some boulders that looked like discarded pieces of masonry, enormous granite and limestone bricks. He led them behind a low hill. When he neared the top, he fell to the ground and stretched out, then cautiously lifted his head and peered over.

Dalila lay beside him. Already she could smell sweet incense and the harsh tang of smoke. She looked over the top of the hill, and what she saw took her breath away. The last time she had entered the temple of Anubis, she had passed through the east entrance. Now she stared at the west facade.

"If we survive this," Meri whispered, "I'm going to have nightmares for the rest of my life."

The giant statues of Anubis stood at the gate. The head of the jackal had red eyes and feral, threatening teeth meant to terrify anyone who saw them. Below the limestone figures stood dozens of priests, holding torches and guarding the huge sandstone pylon. Two towers flanked the monumental gate.

"There's no way," Sudi said. "Shaitan must have figured that we'd come back."

"But how?" Meri asked.

Abdel rested his head in the sand and stared at Dalila. "Enchantress, you must use your power."

Dalila closed her eyes and probed the air, searching for other magic the way her uncle had taught her. Her mind hit something so strong it felt like a slap. Her eyes flashed open, and she jerked back. Cruel magic encircled the front gate, something ancient that tasted of evil. Shaitan had set another trap.

"I can't counter the magic that's surrounding the priests," she whispered. "We're defeated. There's no way we can get inside and steal the magic back."

CHAPTER 21

"Abdel, the infamous tomb robber, is with you," Abdel said. "Pharaohs fear me because I can break in to any tomb. Tunneling into a temple is easy for one who has my talent."

"Temple walls are massive," Dalila cautioned.

"And those in a tomb are not?" Abdel grinned. "I can do it." Without waiting for an answer, he scooted down the hill.

"Let him try," Sudi pleaded. "I want to get back to the party."

"How can you think about partying when we might die any minute?" Meri slid down the slope beside her. "Besides, we don't have a way back."

"If I thought about where we are and what we have to do," Sudi grumbled, "I'd break down and cry. Just let me pretend. All right?"

Dalila sensed that Sudi was on the verge of collapse. "We'll get through this," she said, even though she had too many doubts of her own. She could think of a dozen reasons why Abdel shouldn't try to dig into the temple, but she couldn't come up with a better plan for getting inside.

Abdel led them from the safety behind the hill to the north side of the temple, where deep shadows hid them from the moonlight.

"It's huge," Sudi whispered, gazing up. "It must be nine stories tall."

The wall looked too thick and solid for anyone to break through. But Abdel seemed undaunted. He picked up a sharp rock and scraped it across the surface, testing several places before he found one that suited him. Then he sat down, took a square blade from his pouch, and, using a thin piece of hide, attached it to a sturdy stick. When he was finished, he had a tool that looked like a hatchet. He stood up and struck it against the wall, where it made a huge gash. He smiled gleefully and began his work.

No guards stood near this section of the temple, but that didn't mean spells hadn't been cast. Dalila probed the air for enemy magic, but found none. Apparently even Shaitan believed the temple's walls were impenetrable. Hope grew inside her; maybe they could get inside and steal the magic back after all.

Abdel hacked at the wall until he had hollowed out a place large enough for him to sit in. He crawled inside. The sound of his digging became more muffled as time passed.

When dawn crept over the horizon, Abdel climbed back out, covered with sweat and dust. The blisters on his hands were bleeding. He smiled proudly and bowed, presenting his work for their inspection.

"Wow," Sudi said when she looked inside.

"You're amazing," Meri added with a love-struck look in her eyes.

Abdel beamed.

Dalila held on to Sudi's shoulder and peered into the hole. A huge column stood at the other end of the tunnel, hiding the hole from anyone inside the temple.

"Let me go first." Meri pushed her way between Sudi and Dalila.

Dalila caught her. "I've been thinking about this while Abdel was digging," she said. "I'm going to get the magic back alone. I want the two of you to go home without me."

"No way." Sudi gripped Dalila's hand. "We're not leaving without you."

"Besides," Meri said with her best elfin grin, "we don't have the incantation, so I guess you're stuck with us."

"Find the Hour priests," Dalila instructed. "They must have the incantation. They'll help you get home." She smiled bravely, then ducked into the tunnel and crawled forward, without listening to their arguments. She couldn't say good-bye, because she knew if she did, she'd lose her resolve and cry. She felt certain she'd never see her friends again.

* * *

Cautiously, Dalila slithered out of the tunnel and stood inside the temple. Her fingers grazed the finely painted hieroglyphs on the column. She immediately sensed two forces thrumming around her, filling the air with the static electricity of a dry winter day. Shaitan's magic repelled her, but another, far stronger and older force called to her, luring her forward. She wasn't sure which one she feared more; both meant to destroy her.

Her chest tightened, and her breathing became shallow. She hoped they couldn't sense her presence inside the temple.

As she crept down the corridor, the murmur of voices came from behind her. She flattened herself against the wall, expecting to see mist lazily wending its way toward her, or Shaitan's hateful eyes glaring at her in the gloom.

She edged sideways along the wall. Even though silence filled the corridor, the sense that someone was following her persisted. She didn't have time to play a waiting game to find out who it was.

With silence and stealth, she eased into the next room, then took off, running at full speed, trying to lose whoever was behind her. She dodged into a side chamber and concealed herself behind another pillar.

A soft scratching sound prompted Dalila to peer out. A scribe, lost in concentration, sat cross-legged on the ground, a papyrus unrolled across his lap. He was writing out a list of gifts that had been given to the temple. His palette had six pigment wells and a slot for his reed brushes. More black ink was mixed in a small pot; apparently he had much to write.

Dalila clung to the shadows and quietly made her way past him into the next room; then she hurried on to the darkest part of the temple. The inner sanctuary was near. Her foot hit something solid. A terrible clattering followed. She looked down. Large, unblinking eyes stared back at her, too numerous to count. Dozens of clay statuettes had been left on the floor—substitutes for the worshippers who were unable to visit the temple and give the god daily offerings.

She stepped around them, then pressed her ear against the door to the inner sanctuary. She heard nothing and slipped inside.

Hundreds of oil lamps had been lit; their flames illuminated the huge offering of food that the priests had set out for the god. The room smelled of incense, ripened fruit, and the pungent scent of blue lotus blossoms.

The high priest stood in the very place where the vessel containing the magic had been. He started the ritual cleansing of the statue of Seth. His voice rose in a chant, his tone haunting, the cadence soothing.

Dalila looked around the room. She could feel the entity that existed within the mist beckoning her. It knew she was there, but where was it?

Then she spied an entrance to another room that she hadn't noticed before. She had an idea she'd find the mist there. She stole over to the door and pressed her trembling hand against it, expecting something from the other side to reach out and seize her arm.

When nothing happened, she slowly opened it, and then squeezed inside, closing the door quietly behind her.

She took in a sharp breath

Shaitan stood in front of the gold vessel, staring down at it.

Panicked and desperate, she saw no place to hide. Then, with furtive steps, she moved to a corner and let the shadows swallow her. From there she watched Shaitan, but just as she became confident that he wasn't aware of her presence, he turned abruptly and walked toward her. Terror-stricken, she braced herself, waiting for him to attack.

Instead, he left the room. Evidently he hadn't seen her. A sudden thrill of excitement rushed through her. She had survived one danger; maybe she could survive the next as well. She hurried over to the vessel and looked inside.

The mist was gone.

CHAPTER 22

Dalila swung around, certain it had been a trap. But the doors to the room were closed. The flames in the oil lamps remained still; no sudden draft had disturbed them. Silence prevailed.

She stared back into the empty vessel the way Shaitan had done. Her heart pumped wildly, and her hands felt cold. She didn't know where the mist had gone, but she could feel it stirring the air. Its odd metallic scent wafted over her.

"I'm here," she said, hating her meek tone. She

had meant for her voice to throw the words out in a bold challenge.

A shadow, deeper than the others, spread out against the wall.

With trepidation, she walked over to the pool of black. She almost stepped on it before realizing it was a deep pit. She fell to her knees and looked down. Even in the dim light cast from the flames, she could make out the tunnel at the bottom. It had probably once been intended as a hidden burial chamber for a pharaoh and then abandoned.

"Dalila," a melodious voice called from the tomblike dark. "I knew you would come. I've been impatiently waiting for you."

Then, lithely, the mist spilled from the mouth of the cave, its lustrous glow lighting the darkness. In slow, sinuous curls, it slid up the side of the pit and craftily circled Dalila's wrist, its touch no more than a cold tickle.

Bravely, Dalila flicked it away and remained still, waiting to see what it would do next.

It twittered, scolding her, then stretched until it loomed above her and filled the room with blue light.

No longer contained in the vessel, the mist had grown. Dalila sensed that Shaitan had put it in the pit to give it the freedom to increase its size. She wondered how large and powerful it had become.

Seeming to read her thoughts, it twisted and let itself spread to the ceiling, taking pride in its grandeur, its compelling beauty, its ability to terrify.

She fought back the need to step away and cower at the back of the room. Determined not to show her fear, she straightened her back.

The mist plunged toward her—making her duck and betray herself—then wailed to frighten her more, but Dalila held her ground.

"Come with me," the melodious voice said from the center of the mist. "Come, let me show you what your ancestors had to face."

"But they were successful, weren't they?" Dalila countered in spite of her terror. "They caught and tamed you and made you work for them."

The mist didn't answer, but shrank back until it was no more than a vapor waiting for her at the bottom of the pit.

Dalila stared down at it, undecided. All the

world's creation myths began with emptiness and darkness, but always something within that cosmic void had had the energy to bring forth the universe. What she was looking at now might have been in existence at the beginning: a fragile particle that had spun off from creation in the first explosion. She wondered what power Shaitan saw within her that made him think she could command this magnificent force.

She sensed that it hadn't always been a malicious creature but that somewhere in its desire to escape captivity it had become violent, because it desperately desired its freedom. She wondered who had been the first people to capture and tame it. She imagined her relatives in ancient times, wandering the desert wastelands, pursuing the entity now hidden within the mist below her.

A grating sound pulled her from her thoughts. She twisted her neck to look behind her. The doors swung, still creaking. Someone had just entered the room, but she didn't see anyone attempting to conceal themselves within the shadows. She supposed a draft could have made the doors move, but the strange, prickly feeling of being watched took hold; she knew she wasn't alone. The priests and Shaitan had no reason to hide. Why should they? She was the intruder. Then another thought came to her: maybe they had come to witness her struggle.

She couldn't put off the confrontation any longer. She had to go down into the pit. Besides, what did her own life matter when the future of the world was at stake?

Yet she wasn't going to fight the primordial force as gentle Dalila. She would meet it with fortitude, as the Enchantress. She closed her eyes and prayed to the spirits of her ancestors to give her strength and endurance.

Then, with an incantation spilling from her lips, she stood and stepped off the edge. Her magic defied gravity as she floated down into the darkness, the white linen billowing around her.

"Nice," the voice said. A hand formed in the mist and swirled out. The cold fingers grasped the back of her neck, trying to force her to look deep into the churning vapors.

Dalila averted her eyes. She remembered too clearly how it had hypnotized her before. She spoke the spell for protection, and the orange glow pushed into the mist, surprising it. Spiraling back in a tightening curl, the mist released her.

Even so, she sensed that it hadn't been the power of her magic that had compelled the mist to let her go as much as it had been the mist's own desire to prolong the battle. It wanted to terrify her and quench its need for violence and revenge.

"Do you think the only way I have to hypnotize you is through your eyes?" it whispered seductively, twining around her, its cold seeping down into her bones. A thin layer of frost encrusted her skin where the mist touched her. "I can use your ears as easily as your eyes to entrance and control you."

At once, the tunnel filled with a soft, dreadful thumping. The dull sound vibrated through Dalila.

"The heartbeat of the universe before creation," the dulcet voice explained. "You remember it, Enchantress, don't you?"

Dalila shook her head and tried to focus her mind, but she felt herself weakening. She fumbled through incantations, but the words came out jumbled. Her magic had failed.

"Foolish one," the mist said in a soothing voice. "I had hoped you would recall what you once were. That power. I long to fight it again. Without remembering who you are, what made you think you could come against me?"

"Because it's right," she answered, rubbing her forehead and willing her mind to ignore the steady, thudding beat.

"Because it's right." The voice within the mist repeated her words with utter disdain.

"You don't understand how you're going to be used by Shaitan," Dalila said, speaking in spite of her fear and the growing pain in her head.

Something smacked the ground behind her and drew her attention away from the mist.

The pulsing rhythm stopped, and the mist retreated into the tunnel.

Dalila turned as Sudi tried to slide down the edge of the pit. She hit the bottom and fell forward, landing next to Meri.

"Ouch!" Sudi stood and limped over to Dalila. "It would have been easier if you'd just let us come with you in the first place," she complained.

"All that hiding and following after you was a

major pain." Meri bent over and picked up some objects from the ground.

"You were the ones behind me." Dalila hugged Sudi, but her emotions clashed: she was grateful that her friends had come after her, but she also felt angry that they had; she wanted them to be safe, and they wouldn't be here.

"No way were we going to let you face that mist alone." Meri handed Dalila a reed brush, a pot of black ink, and a roll of papyrus. "I stole these from the scribe, but I spilled some of the ink when I tried to jump down in the pit."

"Why did you steal these?" Dalila asked, baffled.

"Because that dream I had when I got knocked unconscious felt so real," Meri said. "And the woman told me that this was what you needed."

Dalila stared down at the blotches of ink on the papyrus and tried to recall all the incantations that she and Sudi had used to summon Seth.

Most of the spells they had spoken had been incantations to free the force imprisoned within the papyrus. She knew the mist was only a false front created by the true magic; but was it possible that the real force was something so small that it could be suspended in ink and imprisoned in the stroke of a pen on paper?

Her hands began to tremble. She understood at last what she had to do.

CHAPTER 23

The mist seemed to sense Dalila's scheme even before she had the plan clear in her own mind. With a sharp spasm, the vapors pulled back and thickened until it became dense, metallic-looking, a giant silver spear.

"It's going to kill us," Sudi whispered, edging closer to Meri and Dalila.

"No," Dalila answered. "It just wants me." As she spoke, the spear shot toward her, shrieking its fury.

With loud, piercing cries, Sudi charged and

swung, attempting to knock it off course. Then Meri, in a desperate scramble, caught it with her hands. It wrenched free and slammed into Dalila.

The impact threw Dalila back. Her head hit the wall with a sharp crack. Pain spun inside her skull. She gasped and pulled herself up, rubbing the back of her neck.

"How can we fight it?" Sudi stared back at the evil thing, her eyes haunted. "It's like trying to stop a wave in the ocean."

"It feels really creepy, more like frozen slime than mist." Meri spread her fingers and gazed down at the splinters of light stuck in her palms. She shook her hands, and the slivers fell to the ground and dissolved in the dirt. "What is it, anyway?"

"An illusion to hide the real magic," Dalila replied. "The mist is only a sending; something the magic has learned to conjure up in order to hide what it really is."

"So the shadow I saw wrapped around you that night was just another sending," Meri said, her eyes fixed on the brilliance that was getting ready to attack again.

Dalila nodded. "Another form the magic took to protect itself. The shadow fought you just like the mist is fighting us now. When I tossed the papyrus into the water, I freed the real magic."

"It must be incredibly small," Sudi said, "if it was imprisoned in the incantation."

Meri smiled. "Something so tiny it could be captured in the stroke of a pen. That's what the woman in my dream said you had to do."

The mist jounced in front of them, taunting them and gorging itself on their anxiety and fear.

"But how are we going to have enough power to capture it and hold it so Dalila can imprison it in the incantation?" Sudi shook out her arms, getting ready for the next attack.

"Maybe there's a way to make our enemies help us," Dalila said.

Meri whipped around. "You mean Shaitan and Seth?" Her tone implied that she didn't think it was a good idea.

"They want me to use the power within the mist to make a spell to free Seth," Dalila explained. "So that's what I'll do. Once I start writing the incantation, both Shaitan and Seth will send their power to reinforce mine and make sure I'm successful."

Then, rapidly curling into itself, the mist again became a long shaft of silver. It burst through the air, aimed at Dalila. Before she could move, it hit her and splattered into a thousand white sparks. Her head snapped back, and she bit her tongue. Unable to breathe, she collapsed on the ground, her mouth filling with the salty taste of blood.

With an unrestrained cry of joy, the voice within the mist screamed its victory; it had won. It soared high above Dalila before falling back into the darkness. Its unpleasant burbling filled the tunnel.

Dalila tried to rouse herself as Meri sank to the ground beside her.

The light within the pit changed. Dalila knew the mist was preparing for another attack. "I can't survive another blow," she whispered.

Sudi scooted protectively in front of Dalila, shielding her with her body again. "How are you going to get past the mist so you can capture the magic?" she asked.

"We were summoned," Dalila said.

"As if that's going to help us now," Sudi sighed. Her eyes were dull and tired, her spirit crushed.

"We must have supernatural powers," Dalila continued. "Ones we haven't even tested."

"You would think," Meri answered, but there was no optimism in her expression.

Dalila picked herself up. "We must have something strong and powerful within us that we're supposed to use to defend the world against evil."

"Maybe if Abdel—" Sudi began.

"Blaming Abdel won't help us," Dalila said without anger. "We can find a dozen excuses for our failure, but I want to triumph over that . . . that thing."

Sudi nodded.

"So, when it comes at us this time, I want you to cast spells at the mist," Dalila said.

"I don't know that many," Sudi confessed sorrowfully.

"Use your love spell," Dalila said.

"Eeewww!" Sudi squealed.

"Just say anything that will send your magic at

it and distract it," Dalila said. "The spell won't affect it, but it will feel your raw power. Hopefully, that will pull its attention away from me."

"I wish I had your confidence," Meri said.

Another shrill cry resounded through the tunnel.

In the same moment, Sudi raised her hands and with a shaky voice cast the love spell that she had planned to use on Scott. "That he might love me," she finished. Her magic spun inside the mist. The voice within the vapor chuffed in surprise.

Before it could recover, Meri started the spell she sometimes used against Michelle to stop her irritating insults.

"Hotep-ek na," Meri intoned. "May you be at peace with me."

The mist stopped. It became a silver sheet of water that wrinkled and sputtered, then wriggled, clearly agitated, as it tried to shake off Meri's magic.

"That's perfect." Dalila picked up the ink pot, papyrus, and pen. "Keep distracting it with your spells."

As Sudi began again, Dalila jogged into the mist.

It started to push her back, but Sudi's incantation for flawless skin distracted it, and Dalila was able to enter the churning vapors. A deadly cold throbbed through her, but she continued forward in spite of the chill. Magic emanating from within the mist endeavored to twist her thoughts and scramble her intention, but she remained strangely calm. Then, floating in the center, she saw the force behind the magic, a tiny piece of creation no larger than a grain of sand. Its brilliance startled her.

She snatched it from the air. It pricked her skin and tried to burrow into her palm, but she quickly plunked it into the ink and began repeating incantations to imprison it in the clay pot.

Immediately, the mist contracted, swirling down with explosive speed until it was sucked into the black liquid. With the glow from the mist gone, Dalila was surrounded by darkness. She couldn't see to write, but this time childhood memories came to her rescue. She spoke a singsong rhyme that she'd learned on her mother's lap. Instantly, a faint light gleamed over her head.

Meri sat down next to her.

The ink bubbled into seething foam and tried to rise again.

"It's escaping," Sudi said, joining them.

But other energies filled the tunnel: cold, evil forces. Dalila could feel the magic of her enemies surrounding her.

"They're here," Meri muttered under her breath, feeling it, too, "just as you thought. Seth and Shaitan have sent their magic to help you."

The ink settled. Dalila smiled slyly. Seth and Shaitan had power, but not greater than her own. They simply had more experience.

She unrolled the papyrus and dipped her pen into the ink. With one long, graceful stroke, she began, her head bent in concentration. She ignored the throbbing ache in her spine and continued. She was using evil, and there was danger in that, but she also knew that she had no other choice. She might have been the Enchantress, but her power was still a mystery to her.

As her brush scratched across the papyrus, whispers rustled against her ears—the evil voices of Shaitan and Seth, urging her on and sharing their secret incantations to bind the ancient force.

Hours later, when Dalila had finished, she sat back and saw the fear in the faces of her friends, but it was no more than what she felt in her own heart.

"Shaitan will be coming after us now," she warned. "We need to hurry."

Dalila used another incantation to lift herself and her friends from the pit. Then, using speed instead of stealth to make their escape, they all ran through the temple and scrambled into the tunnel that Abdel had dug for them. At last, scorching desert air stung their faces as they fell into the sand, laughing.

Abdel ran toward them, waving his arms.

"He's looks really happy to see us," Meri said.

But Dalila wasn't so sure.

"I think he's trying to tell us something," Sudi said.

"Go back!" Abdel shouted. Something hit him, and he fell to the ground.

Meri rushed to him, and then, sitting next to him, she lifted his head onto her lap.

Dalila joined her. "Is he all right?"

Sudi fell to her knees beside them. She had the

depleted look of someone who was ready to give up. "We did just what Shaitan wanted after all. He'll capture us again, but this time he won't take any chances. We won't get away."

Dalila followed Sudi's tired gaze. Shaitan stood at the far end of the temple, watching them. Even at this distance, Dalila could feel the fiery bloodlust in his eyes, his need to destroy them. Obviously, it was his magic that had attacked and injured Abdel.

She whispered her protective spell, then brought her hand down and sent the orange glow to shelter her friends. She handed the papyrus to Sudi.

Without hesitating, Dalila started forward, determined to fight Shaitan alone.

CHAPTER 24

An apparition, speckled with rainbow lights, spiraled down in front of Dalila. The ghostly image materialized into golden wings curled around a graceful body. When the wings unfolded, the goddess Isis stood before Dalila in her avian form. Her glossy black hair hung over her shoulders.

Abdel tried to get up and run. But Meri caught his wrist, restraining him.

Before Shaitan could throw magic against Isis, she lifted her hand, and sand scudded down the hillside. It blew in front of Shaitan, stopping him.

"Greetings, Sisters," Isis said, glancing back at the storm.

"*Santu!*" Shaitan cursed and called her foul names. "*Tent baiu!*"

Dalila couldn't hear all the words but enough to know he was yelling about slaughtering souls.

Isis seemed pleased that she had vexed him. "My old enemy appears upset."

The goddess turned her attention back to the girls. "You have what Shaitan wants most—the incantation to summon Seth—and, yet, with such a prize, you remain here in the past. Why do you stay?"

"We want to go home," Sudi said. "More than anything, that's what we want to do."

"We don't have the spell for returning to the future," Meri added.

"I gave my magic to the three of you," Isis countered. "The greatest secrets of the universe belong to my Sisters."

"That doesn't mean we know how to use them," Sudi complained.

"The Enchantress does," Isis said.

Dalila bent her head, ashamed, and stared at the sand. She could feel them watching her.

Isis cupped Dalila's chin and forced her to look up. "My scrying glass told me that you would betray me, but now I know your betrayal wasn't as it appeared. To save the world you had to make the incantation to summon Seth. You made the right choice." She looked behind Dalila, seemingly pleased. "And you brought the tomb robber Abdel to me."

"Great Isis." Abdel fell to the ground. "I didn't mean to show disrespect when I broke into the tombs. But the poverty in my village—"

"I'm not going to punish you." Isis spoke with kindness. "I'm going to make you one of my Hour priests."

"Me?" Abdel raised his head, his gaze tentative. "The great and beloved goddess Isis wants the infamous tomb robber Abdel to become an Hour priest?"

Isis laughed. "I need your cunning to outsmart the enemy." Then she faced Dalila again, and even though she appeared angry, the goddess radiated love. "Will it require another death or near-death before you are willing to acknowledge who you are?"

Dalila felt perplexed by her own inability to act. She didn't have an answer.

"How long can you continue to suppress your power?" Isis asked. "Is it worth denying yourself in order to be the person you think other people want you to be? Or are you perhaps afraid that people won't like you if you show them who you truly are?"

"But it's wild and proud and aggressive," Dalila replied. "It's not me at all."

"*It?*" Isis seemed shocked. "You talk as if the Enchantress were another creature, separate from you." She paused. "But then, that is the way you have always treated your true identity, making it something other than yourself."

"Maybe I've neglected it for too long," Dalila replied. She was yearning to give up the masquerade.

"It's time you honored who you really are," Isis said. "The decision is yours alone. Not even my magic can help you."

Dalila nodded. A tear curled down her cheek, and she quickly wiped it away.

"I think I know the incantation for going home," Dalila offered. "I guess I've always known, but I didn't want to seem conceited and—"

"Modesty is so unappealing to me," Isis interrupted. "What good is it if it makes you deny who you are? My Sisters are bold and proud and powerful."

"But what if I'm wrong and only do something more disastrous?" Dalila asked. "I'm scared. I don't want to cause more problems than I already have."

"My husband, Osiris, who is king of the dead, tells me that those who have joined him regret most what they didn't do in life, never their failures, because at least then they tried."

"Take us back," Sudi said. "I don't care if you start acting conceited, like Michelle, or we land in the Potomac. Just take us back and get us away from Shaitan."

Meri seemed perplexed. "If you knew the incantation, then why didn't you use it before?" she asked Dalila.

"Because I wasn't sure," Dalila said, searching

for the right words. "Sometimes it's as hard to admit something magnificent about yourself as it is to confess to a crime." She blushed even as she spoke the words.

Isis smiled and lifted her arms. "You don't need me anymore." She became transparent, her spectral body wavering in the breeze.

"Wait!" Abdel ran after her.

Isis paused, no more than shimmering air.

"How do I find the Hour priests?" Abdel asked.

"You don't need to find them. I will send them to find you," Isis replied. "Many blessings, Sisters," she said before she vanished.

"Can you speak the spell?" Sudi asked.

"I'll try." Dalila checked to make sure that Sudi still held the papyrus in her hands; then she raised her own and opened her palms to the setting sun.

"Wait!" Meri yelled. "Let me say good-bye to Abdel first."

"You'll see him again in a few minutes," Sudi said impatiently.

"But he's crazy in love with me here," Meri countered.

Abdel took Meri's hands. "I vow that I will find a way to see you again in the future, Meritaten, and when I find you, if you don't love me as much as I love you, I swear that I will find a love spell to dominate your heart and make you want me like an ox after grass."

"Like an ox after grass," Meri spat out the words and started laughing.

Abdel looked wounded. "The force of *heka* will make you love me."

"I do love you," Meri said. "I have the biggest crush on you, and you act like I don't even exist. . . . Well, most of the time anyway."

"Impossible." He took her in his arms.

Sudi separated them. "We have to go," she said brusquely.

Abdel kissed the top of Meri's head before he pulled away and darted up the hill.

Dalila began her praises to Amun-Re: *"Neb pet, neb ta, suten maat, neb heh."* When she had finished, she added, "I have walked on thy rays as a lamp under my feet."

The sun seemed to rise. Its dazzling brilliance cracked and split into a thousand golden bricks that came together to form the bridge that spanned time.

"Wow!" Meri cried running onto the bridge. "You've got to show me how to do this. History will be an easy class from now on."

But as soon as Dalila ran up the path toward the future, the bricks buckled. "What's happening?" Meri asked, stretching her arms out for balance.

The bridge shattered. Dalila pitched forward and fell into the sand. Meri and Sudi tumbled after her.

Bricks struck the ground, smashing against one another. They flashed like red diamonds before turning into black stones. Dalila had failed, just as she had feared she would. She and her friends were stranded in the ancient world after all.

CHAPTER 25

"Where are we?" Sudi brushed the sand from her cheeks.

"We never left," Meri said in a small, stunned voice. "Other magic is holding us back. Look behind you."

Dalila sat up, already knowing what she would see. She could feel the disruption of Shaitan's power. Rough, sharp points of magic protruded from the stones and pulsed under his malevolent control.

Shaitan leered at her and walked forward, his hooves silent in the sand. He plucked the papyrus from Sudi's hand, and his cruel expression dared Dalila to stop him. Then he strolled back to the temple, his slowness an insult, expressing his contempt for their power.

"I'm not going to let him win," Dalila said hoarsely. Her throat was still burning from breathing in his magic. In spite of the pain, she forced herself to stand up.

"Be careful," Sudi warned.

But fiery anticipation was already building inside Dalila. She recited an incantation that she had learned from her mother to ward off demons; then she bundled its energy into her hand.

"Sent-na," she yelled at Shaitan. "Fear me."

He swung around.

She threw the magic at him, and the force smashed into his face, making his head jerk back.

Sudi gasped, and Meri cheered.

Dalila braced herself for his counterattack, already deciding on the incantation she would use next. But Shaitan didn't fight her. He stood in the midst of her magic and drew it into his lungs, savoring it, tasting it with the tip of his tongue. His enjoyment was far worse than if he had stormed forward and sent a death hex in retaliation.

Dalila strode toward him, trying to figure out what he was doing; she had not expected this. When she stood in front of him, she snatched the papyrus from his hands and quickly stepped away.

He didn't try to take it back. "Such sweet magic, Dalila," he whispered with a spine-chilling smile. "You don't even know the depth of your power yet. Maybe you should let me show you."

Her skin crawled, and a rush of nausea made her swallow hard. She backed up until she bumped into Sudi.

"He's creeping me out," Sudi said.

"You're not the only one," Meri agreed, pressing against her.

"What a freak," Sudi added. "He looks like he's trying to eat your magic."

Dalila nodded, her uneasiness growing.

"I don't care what he's doing," Meri put in. "At least he's not attacking us. Let's get out of here before he recovers and decides to capture us again."

"Speak the spell," Sudi said.

Dalila faced the setting sun again. As she began her praises to Amun-Re, she looked back over her shoulder to see what Shaitan was doing. Each time she glanced at him, he appeared more defeated. It had to be a ruse, to cover for something treacherous. Her magic, so unpracticed, couldn't have stopped him that easily, and her attack had obviously given him more pleasure than pain.

At last the sun's corona stretched into a thousand tendrils that built a bridge linking the past and the future.

Dalila gingerly tested its strength with her toe before stepping onto it.

"It seems solid enough," Sudi said.

Dalila ventured one last look at Shaitan. He stood motionless, watching her.

"I thought Shaitan was supposed to be stronger than that," Meri said.

"He is," Dalila replied.

"Let's go while he's still caught in your magic," Sudi pleaded, tugging on Dalila's arm. "We can worry about him when we get back home."

The girls raced over the bridge, their feet making a soft, pattering sound.

Dalila envisioned Sara's party: the music, the decorations, the kids dancing.

Sudi sprinted ahead. When she reached the darkness at the other end of the bridge, she screamed, "It's Sara's sweet sixteen!" She whooped and lifted her arms in a sinuous stretch and jumped in with the dancers.

"We're home," Dalila whispered. Her muscles began to relax. Maybe they had defeated Shaitan after all. She felt starved, exhausted, and wonderful. She closed her eyes and let her body find the beat; her hips began to move. She held her hands up and whispered prayers of gratitude.

"Something's wrong." Meri nudged her.

Dalila stopped moving and opened her eyes.

Guys were checking them out. Some had stopped dancing and were goggling at them.

"The linen." Dalila gasped. "It's not transparent, but I don't think it leaves much to the imagination." She gulped and felt herself blush.

"It's no worse than wearing a bathing suit," Sudi said with an audacious smile. Her eyes darted around. She enjoyed the attention. "It just gives a hint of what's underneath."

"That's more than I want to show," Meri said as she tried to hide herself behind Dalila.

Sudi laughed and elbowed her playfully. "You're gorgeous. Flaunt what you've got."

Meri squealed, "For you it's okay, but my mom's running for president."

"Be outrageous. We deserve it." Sudi began dancing again, flirting with the guys and teasing them with her gestures.

Suddenly, Brian was there, a wicked smile on his face. His gaze lingered on Dalila's body, and he didn't bother to hide his attraction. "Did you wear that just for me?" he asked over the music. "You look—" Then, abruptly, he stood at attention, his eyes opened wide, and he had the stunned look of someone who had just been punched in the brain.

He frowned at the line of guys watching Sudi, Meri, and Dalila. "What are you guys gawking at?" he barked. He shoved the one standing nearest him. "Give them some room. Haven't you ever seen belly dancers before?"

Brian kept prodding the onlookers until they formed a circle around the girls. Then he placed two fingers between his lips. His whistle shrilled through the room. The kids standing next to him cringed and covered their ears.

The lead singer motioned to the band to stop playing.

"They're surprise entertainment for Sara," Brian shouted. "Give us the right kind of music. They're here to belly dance."

Dalila smiled and looked at Sudi and Meri.

"Don't tell me Isis is using Brian again," Sudi groaned. Once before, the goddess had entranced Brian and made him help them.

"Isn't it obvious?" Dalila asked.

"I'm glad Isis is using Brian to help us," Meri said, "but I wish she'd given me a shawl. I feel naked." As if in reply, one of the shorter lengths of shiny fabric fell to the floor in front of her. She quickly wrapped the silver material around her body.

"Is there any doubt now that the goddess is using Brian to provide us with an excuse for being so scandalously dressed?" Dalila circled her wrists, raising her hands above her head. She held the papyrus in her right hand. With her left, she lifted the little and index fingers into the graceful position she had been taught. Then, stretching her body seductively, she gave her audience a sultry look and waited for the music to begin again.

"Let's get with it!" Brian yelled.

The bass guitar began playing a Middle Eastern rhythm. The drummer joined in, pounding out the backbeat. Dalila could feel the anticipation in the kids who were watching her, and that made her want to give them her best performance ever. As the melody began flowing, so did her arms, in graceful, snaky movements. She shimmied before doing smooth figure eights with her hips. Girls watched, wiggling their bodies, trying to figure out how she was able to move so gracefully.

Sudi and Meri joined Dalila, swaying along with her, their bellies undulating.

Other dancers twisted and squirmed, trying to imitate Dalila. Even the guys shook their shoulders. Mostly, they bounced and frolicked, their angel wings flapping wildly.

"I love your surprise!" Sara screamed. She spun in between Sudi and Dalila and twirled with them, her black cape billowing out. "Thank you.

You've made the party memorable. No one will ever forget it."

"We didn't do it," Sudi said. "It was your idea. All your work and planning made the party magical."

Unexpectedly, Abdel pushed through the dancers. His smile was huge. He wrapped his arms around Dalila and gave her a friendly hug. "I knew you had returned, so I got over here as quickly as I could." His hair was wet from the shower, and he smelled of soap.

"We know all about you now," Sudi said, embracing him dearly. "Abdel, the infamous tomb robber."

He blushed.

Meri grabbed his arm, forcing him to turn and face her. "Like an ox after grass?" Meri teased, repeating the words he had spoken to her in ancient Egypt. She gave him an impish grin.

"The words were appropriate for the time, Meritaten." He gazed down at her, no longer hiding his affection.

He returned his attention to all three girls. "Do you understand now why I couldn't give you any guidance?"

"No!" Meri, Sudi, and Dalila shouted.

"If you had told us how to deal with Shaitan, it would have been a lot easier," Meri said.

"But if I had told you what to do, then you might have done something differently, and you wouldn't have been able to capture Shaitan," Abdel said as a train of dancers crowded in front of Dalila and separated her from her friends.

"We didn't capture him!" Dalila yelled.

She tried to catch up to Meri and Abdel, but the arms and legs of the dancers bumped against her and she remained lost behind the bobbing heads and gyrating hips. Did Sudi and Meri think that the spell Dalila had cast over Shaitan had somehow kept him mesmerized, captive in the ancient land? Dalila was certain that it hadn't. She had a bad feeling that she had lingered too long at the party. She should have immediately taken the incantation and put it with the Book of Thoth, where it would have been safe. The truth weighed on her. She had stayed because she had hoped to see Carter, and that foolish mistake might have cost her everything. She rushed back to Sudi.

Scott was standing with her now, cradling her in his arms.

"What was that bridge outside?" Scott asked as Dalila approached them. "I asked Sara, but she said she didn't have any plans for it."

"Just an illusion," Sudi lied, "but it didn't work too well, so we decided to belly dance."

"Your trick fooled me." Scott pulled Sudi closer. "But I'm glad you decided to dance instead."

"Sudi." Dalila tried to get her attention, but Sudi was too busy kissing Scott to hear anyone.

Maybe it was better to act alone, anyway. Dalila hurried toward the exit.

When she neared the stage, Michelle stopped her. "I can't believe you did that to me."

"What?" Dalila asked.

Her concentration abruptly shifted from Michelle's scowl to a peculiar crackle in the air. Her skin felt as if nettle hairs were brushing over her. She rubbed her arm.

"You know exactly what I mean," Michelle continued. "You convinced the party planner to cancel my performance so that you could hog all the attention for yourself."

"That's not true," Dalila said.

"I won't forget this," Michelle threatened.

Some of the kids had stopped dancing and were looking around, aware of the change in the atmosphere and trying to figure out what was causing the strange, stinging sensation. But their fears weren't focused on the supernatural; this was D.C., and they had daily reminders of the possibility of another terrorist attack.

Dalila pushed around Michelle. She needed to find Abdel.

"You can't just walk away from me." Michelle stomped after her.

The band stopped playing. The houselights came on, and beneath the garish lighting, the faces of the partyers looked afraid. Security guards and the Capitol police had suddenly appeared and were walking through the crowd, trying to calm everyone.

Sudi broke away from Scott and ran over to Dalila. "Is Shaitan doing this?" she asked with a worried look.

"Excuse me," Michelle said, annoyed. "I haven't finished my conversation with Dalila."

Sudi ignored Michelle and went on, "We have

to do something before everyone bolts and stampedes toward the exit."

"We need a distraction." Dalila turned to Michelle. "It's time for you to get on stage and do your Happy Birthday rap."

Michelle looked startled. Then her eyes narrowed. "Why now, all of a sudden?" she asked suspiciously.

"We couldn't let you overpractice and lose all your energy," Dalila lied, trying to sound convincing. "That's why we told the party planner to make you stop. You needed to save some energy for your real performance."

Michelle beamed. "Thanks."

She ran onto the stage and took the microphone. Feedback screeched, and everyone grabbed their ears. The piercing sound broke the tension; kids laughed, glad to release their nervousness.

"This is my special Happy Birthday tribute to Sara," Michelle yelled. Then she clapped her hands high over her head, urging everyone to join in.

Meri elbowed her way between two guys who were laughing at Michelle. "We've been trying to find you," she said when she was finally standing next to Dalila and Sudi.

Abdel followed her. He looked troubled. "Where is the incantation?"

Dalila held up the papyrus.

"We need to put it with the Book of Thoth," Abdel said. "But someone must remain here in case Shaitan decides to do something. His magic is in the air. I assume he's using it to find the incantation."

"I'll take the papyrus to your house," Dalila suggested.

"Take Sudi with you," Abdel said. "Meri and I will stay here."

As Dalila turned to leave, she bumped against Brian's broad chest.

"Come on with me. You need a ride." Brian tore off his angel wings and began marching toward the exit.

Sudi and Dalila exchanged quick glances. "Isis is using Brian again," Dalila said. "The goddess has provided us with a chauffeur to take us to Abdel's."

As Brian plowed ahead, Scott began walking with Sudi and Dalila. "Are you going to do that stairway-to-heaven trick again? I want you to show me how you created the illusion and made the bridge. It's fantastic."

Brian stopped. "You can't go with us, Scott," he said gruffly.

Scott looked from Brian to Sudi, puzzled. "Why are you going to show Brian and not me?"

"Just get over it, Scott," Brian blustered. "Sudi's still crushing on me."

"That is so not true." Sudi swung at Brian, but he jumped back, and her fist hit only air.

"Look at the pathetic way she uses any excuse to touch me," Brian boasted. "Sorry about that, Scott, but you don't stand a chance with me around."

Dalila blocked Sudi before she could throw another punch.

"I have got to talk to Isis," Sudi said glumly as they stepped outside into the cold night air. "She needs to know that Scott can drive, and he has a better car."

Brian's Cadillac was noisily idling near the entrance, its parking lights blinking. Brian walked over to the driver's side and slid behind the steering wheel.

"There must be something about Brian that makes him easy for Isis to use." Dalila climbed into the front seat and scooted over to give Sudi room.

"Yeah," Sudi smirked. "He's as dumb as a—" The car took off. She jumped in, and, after she had fastened her seat belt, she leaned out and closed the door.

Brian drove down the wrong side of the street, to avoid hitting people in the crossing lane.

"Is there a reason for us to hurry?" Dalila gripped the edge of the seat.

"I'm trying to beat the devil," Brian snorted.

"Do you think that was Isis speaking through him?" Sudi asked.

"I don't know," Dalila said. "But I hope she's the one doing the driving."

Brian ran a red light, and a taxicab swerved to avoid crashing into the Cadillac. Horns blared, but Brian didn't slow down. He pressed his foot on the accelerator, and the car sped forward.

Dalila hid her eyes.

Minutes later, the car fishtailed around a

corner in Georgetown, then stopped, with a squeal of brakes, in front of Abdel's house. The smell of burned rubber wafted into the air.

Dalila let her hands fall from her face. She didn't like what she saw. Shaitan sat on the porch steps. Zack and his two friends lolled against the railing.

"Why is Shaitan waiting outside?" Sudi asked Dalila. "I was afraid he'd be inside, ready to ambush us, but it doesn't make sense that he'd be out here."

"His evil is too strong," Dalila answered. "The ancient spells that guard the Book of Thoth protect the house as well and repel Shaitan. He'd have to enter with one of us so that the old magic would think he was invited. I assume that's why he's waiting." Suddenly Dalila knew what she had to do to stop Shaitan, but she needed to do it alone.

"How are we going to get past them so we can go inside?" Sudi asked.

"Sweet damn," Brian said unexpectedly, distracting them from Shaitan.

"What now?" Sudi asked, exasperated.

"I love a fight more than anything." Brian

opened the car door. "And I smell a real brawl: four guys just waiting for my fist."

Dalila and Sudi scrambled out of the car and ran after him, trying to hold him back.

"Zack," Brian called out. "You're in their way. They want to go inside." Brian flexed his muscles, getting ready to bulldoze Zack.

"Hey, Brian." Zack seemed uncertain. He had obviously expected an encounter with magic, not fists, and not with Brian.

The other two guys straightened, intimidated by Brian's swagger, and glanced at Shaitan for guidance.

Shaitan stood up, suddenly the peacemaker, and spoke to Zack. "Maybe we should leave now."

Brian looked disappointed, but he didn't drop his threatening pose. He waited until they had vanished from view.

"I can't believe they're going to go away," Sudi whispered.

"Luck is with us," Dalila said. "Above all else, the cult must protect its true identity. The members can't afford public exposure, and a fight with Brian would definitely do that. Didn't you say Brian's father was a general who worked at the Pentagon?"

Sudi nodded.

When they reached the door, Dalila stopped. "Go on back to the party," she said to Sudi. "I'll be all right."

"Don't you want to go with us?" Sudi asked.

"Why would she?" Brian spoke up. "Carter's not there."

"Having fun is not always about guys, Brian," Sudi said.

"That from you!" Brian made a face.

"Please!" Dalila interrupted their argument. She needed to be alone for her plan to work. "I just want to go home after I finish here."

But Sudi looked doubtful. "I don't like leaving you by yourself."

"I'm all right," Dalila said.

"I'll call you tomorrow, then." Reluctantly, Sudi headed back to the car with Brian.

"You know, Sudi," Brian said in a serious tone, "maybe if you would mess around with Scott it would help you get over me."

Sudi yanked the car door open. "Brian, you're a meathead," she said before sliding inside.

"You're making me totally pissed," Brian said as he started the engine. The Cadillac lurched forward.

Dalila waited until she could no longer hear the car. Then she cast a simple spell. The dead bolt clicked. She entered the house and stepped into the dark living room, leaving the door open behind her. Immediately, she discerned a change in the night. Her arms prickled. Her skin stung.

A sudden gust slammed the door against the wall and knocked her to the floor. The papyrus slipped from her hand. She stretched out her arm, trying to grab it back, but the wind blew the papyrus farther away.

Shaitan hovered, a ghost in front of her, before he let his body form. His hooves echoed hollowly on the floorboards as he walked over to the papyrus. His yellow eyes shone triumphant in the dark.

"The goddess Isis puts too much trust in your skills, Enchantress. Your magic is powerful, but your experience is weak. You should have suspected that you had won too easily." He bent over to pick up the papyrus.

Dalila lunged forward and grabbed his wrist. "And you should have suspected that I left the door open and allowed you to enter Abdel's house," she countered. "Abdel's house is filled with protective magic. You won't be as strong here as you are on the street."

He didn't seem concerned. "You've proven yourself worthy, Enchantress. You've done exactly what I needed. The primal magic is imprisoned in the incantation, a slave now, that will do my bidding when I intone the spell and summon Seth."

He bent over to collect the papyrus.

Dalila smiled darkly and let the Enchantress rise inside her. The tips of her fingers pulsed with mysterious light as she slammed her power at him.

Shaitan straightened up and caught the magic. He was bewitched by it, but not harmed. "I let you leave the ancient world so I could speak to you alone and make my offer. Become my queen of evil," he said. "I could teach you so much. With your power and my skill, we wouldn't need Seth to bring a reign of darkness to the world. We could do it on our own."

Then, without speaking a spell or moving his

hand to summon energy, his magic came at her, an invisible wave, not to hurt her but to show off his strength. The air fondled her and caressed her hair, then lifted her three inches off the floor before gently setting her back down.

"Apparently, the ancient spells within this house don't have that much power over me after all," he said, pleased with his display.

"But I do," Dalila said. An aura of shimmering light encircled her. In its glow, Shaitan looked more demon than human.

He closed his eyes, waiting to feel her magic again. "Enfold me in your enchantment."

Dalila invoked a spell, but not one she had learned as a child. This one she had taken from the Book of Thoth, an ancient curse that Horus had used against Seth. "*Sebau xer*," she shouted. "The evil one has fallen."

Shaitan's eyes flashed open. The air convulsed around him. He fell to his knees with a heavy thump. This time he tried to send magic against her, but her power held him back. Blue sparks crackled over the tips of his fingers, then fell to the floor, a pile of ash. He stared down at the magic in stunned silence. A spasm rushed through his body, and he was forced down on his hands and knees, bowing before her.

"We are not finished, Enchantress," he threatened, but it was too late.

Dalila waved her hand, and he vanished, captured for now in her spell.

Stillness returned to the room. She carried the papyrus upstairs and left it on the table in the small room where Abdel kept the Book of Thoth.

Then she hurried back down the steps and outside into the chill night air. She closed the door behind her, eager to get home.

At the corner, a lone figure stood under the streetlight, waiting for her.

CHAPTER 26

Carter walked slowly toward Dalila, gazing tenderly into her eyes. When he reached her, he slipped his hand around her waist and pulled her to him.

A jolt of pleasure rushed through her. She lifted her arms and let her hands rest on his shoulders, then waited, anticipating his kiss.

He pressed against her, warming her body with his own. His lips moved over her cheek to her ear. "I love you, Dalila," he whispered, but his tone was filled with sadness. "When I joined the cult, I didn't think their magic was real. I was looking for fun. By the time I figured out what they were really about I was in too deep—"

"I'll help you get out." Her words came quickly. "I don't care what your past has been."

"It's not my past," he whispered back. "The cult is my future."

"No," she said. She had felt frightened when she faced Shaitan, but this fear was worse. Her stomach knotted. She couldn't lose Carter.

"There's no way they'll let me go now," he said. "It's impossible."

"They can't force you," she said.

"They can, and they are," he replied.

"But why? How?" Her mind reeled, trying to come up with a possible reason.

"It's too dangerous for us to be together," he continued, without answering her question. "That's why I'm telling you good-bye."

She clutched his hand. How could she care for him so much, especially knowing that he had chosen to remain a member of the cult whose leaders wanted her dead?

He pulled his hand away and started walking away from her.

She began shivering, but not from the cold. She glanced up at the stars and held her hands open to receive their power. Silver sparkles filled her palms. She spoke ancient words over the starry light and then threw it at Carter.

When it touched his back, he turned. Her spell fell to the ground, a smear of silver on the sidewalk.

Her heart was racing. She willed him to rush back to her and pull her into his arms again.

But he remained firmly rooted to the spot, the light from her magic casting an eerie glow across his face. "Your love spell won't work on me, Dalila, because I already love you."

"What you're doing is wrong!" she screamed.

The roar of a car engine startled her. Headlights blazed over her as the huge Cadillac squealed to a stop. Meri and Sudi jumped out and ran to her.

"Brian said you needed us," Meri said, her eyes searching for the danger. "We figured Isis was using him again."

"He said you'd been hurt," Sudi said.

"I was," Dalila said miserably. "Carter broke my heart." She bit her lip to keep from crying.

"Is that him?" Sudi didn't wait for an answer. "Carter, you promised me on our friendship that you wouldn't hurt Dalila."

He lifted a hand and waved. "It's for her own good," he shouted back.

Sudi looked at Dalila, seeking an explanation.

"He was right to break up with me," Dalila said.

"Why?" Meri asked.

Dalila shrugged and locked Carter's secret deep inside her. "I don't want to talk about it yet."

"Come on." Sudi put her arm around Dalila. "If there's one thing I know, it's how to mend a broken heart. A party with friends is the only cure."

Meri linked arms with Dalila, the three girls walked back to the Cadillac. "We'll dance away the pain."

Dalila pulled them closer to her. "You're the best Sisters anyone could ever have." She let Meri and Sudi climb into the car ahead of her while she gazed up at the stars.

"I vow by your light that Carter will be my

first love and my last." The oath gave her strength, and then she sent other words out into the night to Carter. "I'm the Enchantress, and nothing can be denied me. I'll have you someday, Carter. I don't know when or how, but I will."